USA TODAY BESTSELLING AUTHOR

Dale Mayer

Bonaparte's BELLE

HEROES FOR HIRE

BONAPARTE'S BELLE: HEROES FOR HIRE, BOOK 24
Dale Mayer
Valley Publishing Ltd.

ISBN-13: 978-1-773364-11-7
Print Edition

Books in This Series:

About This Book

Sheriff Angela Zimmerman is not what Bonaparte expects when he arrives in her district. But he was here to help her out at Levi's request. A little matchmaking by Levi was going on too but didn't change the fact that she was in trouble.

When Levi said he was sending a man over, she didn't realize he meant this gentle mountain of a man. Still Bonaparte was confident and capable, and that's what mattered. Something rotten was happening in her town, and getting to the bottom of it alone was nearly impossible. Especially when all her deputies had been coerced to quit.

Sensing something much bigger was going on is one thing, but proving it is another. So the two set out to get the proof they need—no matter the danger. No one expected what they found …

Sign up to be notified of all Dale's releases here!
https://smarturl.it/DaleNews

Prologue

BONAPARTE GASPARDE WAS happy for Zack and Zadie. It's not what he had expected when they'd started this mission, but, once he'd seen the sparks flying between the two of them, he knew there would be no other way for this to end. Zack looked like he had a whole new lease on life, and Bonaparte was happy for his friend.

Bonaparte had returned to the United States with them and had spent a few weeks lost, until Levi suggested he stay and do a couple jobs, at least until he figured out what he wanted to do, now that he hadn't upped again in the navy.

Being here was hard in a way. His introspection into his prior relationship was brutal. Yet he'd seen so many beautiful couples at Levi's place that Bonaparte wondered if he was half inclined to stick around in case some of that pixie dust might fall his way.

Just then Levi walked into the kitchen. "Hey, how are you doing? Everything okay?"

"I'm good," Bonaparte said.

"So how do you feel about heading outside of Denver to help out a friend?"

"What's going on there?" he asked.

"Another case gone wrong." Levi sighed, as he sat beside Bonaparte. "Actually a favor for the sheriff of a small town."

"What kind of a problem? Need a bodyguard or what?"

"Oh no, nothing like that," he said. "The sheriff just needs someone to deputize for the short-term, having told the town that new staff was on the way, so they're expecting somebody, yet nobody is actually coming."

"What, so I'd be like a relief deputy for what? A week or two?" He shrugged. "I've never been in that role before, but how hard can it be? I'm game."

"Yeah, but you're walking into a trap," Levi said. "It was one of reasons for saying backup was coming, but it's also the reason it hasn't happened. It's a dangerous situation, and anybody the sheriff brings in could have their hands full."

"Great," Bonaparte said, straightening up with a big grin. "Sounds like my kind of job. Who's the sheriff?"

"Her name is Angela Zimmerman," Levi said. "She's hell on wheels and happens to be an old friend, so do what you can to keep her alive."

"A female sheriff, sounds like fun."

"Angela is good people. She comes down on the side of right every time."

Bonaparte pursed his lips. He had no reason not to go. In fact, it would be better than sitting here and reviewing his failed relationships.

"Listen. Don't let one poisonous nutcase spoil you for all the beautiful flowers out there."

Bonaparte laughed at that. "I doubt that Ice would appreciate being called a flower, and I sure don't see my ex-wife like that."

"So true," Levi said, with a grin. "And good on the ex. Now go give Angela a hand." He stood, and they shook hands. "At the bare minimum, this job should keep you busy, and I know you always love helping the underdog. I can guarantee you that Angela needs help."

"Well, when you put it that way, how can I refuse?"

Chapter 1

BONAPARTE FOLLOWED LEVI'S directions, including picking up a special truck, suitable for the would-be deputy, waiting for him at the airport. Once he left the city limits of Denver, he headed for the small town to meet Sheriff Angela Zimmerman. It was a heck of a name. He wanted to call her Angel or Angie, but Levi had warned him that she wasn't a nickname kind of person.

On the whole trip, Bonaparte had been wondering if that meant she wasn't the warm or cuddly type. He didn't know why the hell he was even thinking along those lines anyway. Deb, his ex, had been very cuddly. She was the kind of small bundle who liked to sit in his lap and just curl up and snuggle. But she hadn't been all that great at getting up when work was to be done. She had been all about being the little princess, not so much about being a partner. But they had two wonderful kids, and he enjoyed every freaking minute he had with them.

They would be coming in another few weeks for the summer holidays, and that was something he had to figure out too. Having left the navy, he found a house not too far from the compound that he would share with his kids. But, so far, Bonaparte had just been enjoying time with Levi and his crew. And now Bonaparte was heading to this job, where he would be deputized, ... whatever the hell that would mean.

When he pulled into town and found the sheriff's office just on the side of the street, he turned and parked, then hopped from his truck. A black half-ton pickup, it was dusty as hell. He shook his head. He would wash it very soon. It wasn't good for a vehicle to be covered like it was. He normally took really good care of his equipment, and he hated to see something like this sit around dirty.

He hitched up his jeans and took a slow look around. There was a problem all right, but he hadn't been given too many details, just that Angela needed help and somebody she could trust. Well, he was trustworthy; she could count on that. If Angela came down hard on the side of right, then he would be right there with her. He kicked a rock out of the way and walked slowly up the long wooden steps to the big veranda out front. There was a very western look to the area, which surprised him. He walked into the office and stood there at the entrance. Not a soul to be found. He took a few steps forward, surprised that the door was even unlocked when empty, when a thirtysomething woman rushed out of the back, a beaming smile on her face.

"Sir, may I help you?"

"I'm here to see the sheriff," he said, in a slow drawl, his hands on his hips as he studied her.

"Angela," she said, with a nod. "Hang on a moment." She disappeared into an office down at the end of the hallway. A few minutes later she rushed back out and smiled at him.

"She'll be out in a minute." She motioned at the hard bench along the front window. "Feel free to take a seat."

He looked at her and nodded.

He didn't move; he just stood here, studying his surroundings. He was a big man, which was an understatement, and he had a tendency to dwarf everything around him. However, this office was mostly empty, with just the odd desk here and there, so it felt spacious and comfortable. Its old worn hardwood floor had seen more than a few people tread its wooden surface.

When the sound of a long-legged clip came toward him, he raised his head, and one eyebrow shot up. Angela had to be at least six feet tall. Long, lean, with an almost raw-boned look. But her skin was fresh, the look in her eyes direct and level. And, if she had long hair, it was hard to see because it was kept back in a clip at her neck.

He smiled at her and said, "Bonaparte. At your service."

Her eyebrows shot up. "Wow," she said, "follow me, please." Angela ignored the curious gaze from the woman sitting at the front desk, watching their every move. Angela immediately pivoted on her heel and walked back to her office. He followed the jean-clad figure, wondering what would put a woman like her in the office of county sheriff in the first place and, more important, what kind of trouble she could be in.

As she walked into her office, she held the door open for him. When he stepped in, she pointed at the visitor's chair and closed the door with a sharp *click* behind him. Then she walked around her desk, sat down, and pushed a button on a small machine to her side.

He looked at it, then at her, his gaze hardened. "A frequency jammer? Are you really expecting that level of trouble?"

Her gaze was equally hard, and she gave a clipped nod. "Yes."

As soon as the buzzer on the machine stopped, she nodded, pushed it off to the side, then settled back and interlocked her fingers, while she studied him.

He waited. If she wanted to play that game, he could too.

"Did Levi tell you what's going on here?"

"Not exactly, no. Levi said that you were in trouble, that you were an old friend, and that you were somebody who firmly came down on the side of right," he said, paraphrasing. "I do too. So, if you need help, I'm here."

"And just you?"

He gave her a wolf of a smile. "Just me."

Her grin was almost as feral, as she looked at him and nodded. "Okay," she said, "in that case, I'll accept it gratefully."

"Where are your deputies?"

"Run off," she said. "Every one of them threatened, their families threatened as well."

He stared at her in shock.

She nodded. "I've contacted the sheriffs in two neighboring counties. Both of them told me to lay low and to not cause any trouble. And that they'd been threatened as well."

"Did you go above them?"

"No," she said. "Nobody here likes a woman sheriff to begin with."

He settled back with a nod. "So you don't want to give in."

"Would you?"

"Well, it would never have happened to me," he said.

Her gaze narrowed, and then she gave a nod again. "It's sexist, but that's true. It wouldn't," she announced. "But I don't think you're the kind who would let anybody run you out of town either."

"No, not likely. What kind of trouble?"

"What kind of trouble do you want?" she said bluntly. "It's all here."

"It looks like such a small sleepy town," he said, with a drawl.

She laughed. "Actually it is. Or it was. Until some wannabe badasses moved in and started terrorizing everybody."

"And you can't throw them in jail?"

"Well, I would if I could get some actual evidence, but these two have a lot of friends and access to a lot of money. So the town is terrified of them, and I've been warned to just get up and leave or else."

"But that's not your style."

"Not mine, not yours, not Levi's."

"Good enough," he said. "Okay, what do we need to do to get evidence, so we can pick up these guys and toss them in the clink?"

"If we toss them in the clink, we better have enough evidence to hold them because they'll be lawyered up and shouting for bail within minutes."

"And what kind of bail are we talking about here?"

"If they've done what I think they've done, I'd like to see it go as high as one million dollars."

He let out a slow whistle. "So, murder?"

"Yes," she said, her voice gentling. "Murder."

"Of whom?"

She opened a drawer on the side and pulled out a file about one-quarter-inch thick. She flipped it open and handed him the clipped papers from the top. "Here's a copy of the notes I have so far," she said. "These are cases involving people I can connect to them, ... in theory at least. Two are my best bets. This operation has been going on locally for over a year."

"But no proof?"

"Not enough," she corrected. "This has to be a locked-down airtight case."

"And these are all …" He looked at the photos and said, "They're all old people."

"They are, indeed, and, in all cases, these are people who stood in the way in some fashion."

"These guys wanted their properties?"

"I don't know whether they are after the properties, the businesses, or the land. It's not as if they're talking. But they've done this before. They've gone into various towns, bought up a lot of land, razed a lot of old homesteads, and put in modern facilities."

"And is your town against that?"

"Not at all," she said, "except that most of the people involved weren't interested in selling. One was and he's alive still, in a nursing home." She nodded at the faces in photos he held. "None of the others wanted to. Not a one."

He frowned, as he continued to look at the photos. "Money usually talks, and, if these assholes have money, why wouldn't they have tried that?"

"All of the deceased were born here," she said, "and spent their whole lives in those homes."

"So couldn't these guys just have outwaited them?"

"Did I tell you that they were young? Like, I mean, they're young. As in, they have absolutely no intention on waiting for anybody to die of natural causes before they can implement their plans."

"And I suppose young and wealthy goes along with cocky and arrogant?"

"Absolutely," she said, and she laughed. "Sounds like

you understand the problem already."

"Oh, hell yeah," he said. "We've seen guys like this before. Generally they're not as well organized though, and don't move from town to town."

"I think they work on a premise of fear and intimidation," she said. "What I haven't figured out yet is what they want to do with these properties. Because, so far, nothing's happening, other than a direct geographical connection to three parcels."

"Same thing in the previous towns?"

"I don't know that the previous properties were geographically connected. Need to check that out. Their MO has been to buy up all the properties they could, and, some of which they're just sitting on. It doesn't make a whole lot of sense, except that it's all really prime real estate. Some are off the highway just out of town, like a place you'd see a large diesel gas station or something like that. But that takes money too."

"But you said they have money?"

"Sure. They certainly seem to, but I don't know whether they have millions, billions, or trillions at this point in time," she said, with a wave of her hand.

"I'll look into their portfolio and see just where they're at," he said, pulling out the sheet with the list of the names. "Brothers?"

"Yes," she said. "And their father was Marcus Gapone." At that, Bonaparte lifted his gaze and stared at her in shock. She nodded. "Yeah, one of the notorious crime bosses. These two cut their teeth on that shit, and now they're here in my town."

"Wow," he said, settling back. "When you bite into trouble, you really take a big bite, don't you?"

"I've never been one to walk a fine line of niceties," she said, "but I've always been fair. These people make my skin crawl. And make me pissed off and angry."

"You know that they won't go down easy, right?"

"Of course I do. And I also know that they'll do everything possible to slide their way out of it. So we either get that evidence we need, or it's a lost cause."

"Even with the evidence," he said, "don't count on any witnesses because they'll pressure them into not testifying."

"I know," she said. "I have my suspicions that they have experience with witness intimidation in the past. Potentially with deaths occurring."

He whistled. "Are you working with anybody else on this?"

She shook her head. "I've kept it very close to the vest, up to this point."

"Is that because you don't want anybody else to know because you're afraid somebody will do something to you or because you don't know who to trust?"

She laughed, but it was a bitter sound. "All of the above."

ANGELA STUDIED THE man in front of her. The photo Levi had sent her one year ago didn't do him justice. He was a monster of a man—but with a sense of purpose, a sense of assurance that he could handle whatever went wrong in his world. A part of her wished she had the same sense. But something about being targeted and having her entire staff walk out definitely left her sitting here, realizing just how vulnerable she really was. But instead of making her even more afraid, it just pissed her off so much more.

When she had finally broken down and told Levi what the hell was going on here, he had suggested that Bonaparte come and give her a hand. She wasn't sure why he had been chosen, but, as she saw the mountain of a man in front of her, she wasn't at all unhappy with Levi's choice. She should have let Levi introduce them a long time ago, when he'd first brought it up, but she'd put it down to Levi's matchmaking.

Now she needed this man for a whole different purpose. The man looked like he hated all kinds of injustice and would go to bat for any underdog. If she needed one thing right now, it was somebody strong at her side. A set of brains to give her a hand to figure this out was nice too.

"I really didn't know what to do," she said. "And, when you don't have a way forward, you flail around, standing in place."

"Or you stand your ground," he said gently, "until you figure it out."

"Sure, until suddenly you don't have enough time to figure it out because they've already come after you."

"In that case," he said, "if you think an attack is imminent, how prepared are you to defend this location?"

"They won't come in a frontal attack," she said, leaning back in her big office chair. She picked up a pen and flipped it through her fingers. "The deputies were each contacted at home. By somebody who doesn't live here, offering money to stay quiet or punishment if they didn't. But the punishment wasn't to be done to them directly, it was directed to family members with a promise of more, forcing the deputies to understand just what would be done."

"Of course, attack where it hurts the most. Target the loved ones."

She said, "Doing it that way makes people far more malleable than if they were roughed up themselves."

"And do you have the same weakness?"

She looked at him in surprise. "Weakness?"

"Is there somebody you love—they can manipulate, kidnap, or torture—in order to force you into doing what they want?"

"No," she said shortly. "There isn't, and that's causing them some trouble."

"Well then, the really simple answer for them is just to remove you from the issue altogether."

"Indeed," she said, with a hard smile. "And, as long as I'm in the sheriff's office, that's a little hard to do." He looked around and saw the bedroll on the floor in the corner and a small bag on top of it. "You're sleeping here?"

"My vehicle had a brake issue," she said shortly. "It's taking a while to get fixed. And I'm not sure I'll trust it then."

"Shit," he said. "What about your house? Where is it, and what does it look like?"

"It's a rancher on some acreage about ten miles from here," she said.

"Nice," he said. "No parents living with you, no children, no siblings?"

She shook her head. "No, no, and no."

"Wouldn't it be easier to defend your own home?"

"Maybe, but the brakes didn't get me home," she said. "They only got me to here."

"I didn't see a vehicle out front, did I?"

"It's in the shop."

"Right. When's it due to be ready?"

"Supposedly this afternoon."

"Plan of action?"

"I'm working on it," she said. Then she shook her head and tossed down the pen. "But I'm not getting very far."

"Sounds to me like we have some work to do," he said and pulled his chair closer, dropping the file on her desk from his side and reaching across for an empty pad of paper sitting off to her side. Snagging it, he said, "Now let's get some of this shit figured out."

He couldn't even believe what he had heard so far, and a slow burn had started in his belly. "What threats have you had?"

"Notes left under the door, here at work, at my home, and in my vehicle," she said. Opening a drawer to the left of her, she pulled out an envelope and quickly upended it.

He grabbed a pencil, and, using the eraser end, he quickly shuffled them back and forth. "Did you get them checked for fingerprints?"

"I did," she said. "Nothing."

He read them slowly. "*Get out of town, bitch. Being a sheriff isn't a woman's position!* So ... threats, but not too-too bad."

"No," she said. "Just bad enough."

"Exactly." He frowned. "Anything else?"

"A couple of dead rats on the front step."

He raised an eyebrow at that. "So that could be related or maybe not."

"Exactly."

"But nobody's tossed any dead pets at you or anything else like that?"

"No," she said, settling back. "I have three dogs at home though, and that's a concern."

"Watchdogs?"

"One, the other two are wannabes," she said, with a

crooked smile.

"Good. And what about your receptionist out there?"

"Lana? She's been here for over a decade, and she doesn't believe there's any threat at all."

"Is that credible?"

"Not in my book," she said, "but nobody really believes me, and the other deputies won't even admit to it."

"Anything else?" he asked, looking at her.

She shrugged. "No. I don't think so."

"You don't *think* so?" he said, with emphasis. "What about on your phone? Anything there?"

She shrugged. "Yeah, definitely had a few odd calls."

"Anybody you know?"

"No. Most people in town know me, and I know most of them," she said. "I was born and raised here, so most of them are … most have been reasonable."

"But some of them haven't been," he pounced.

"Some of them haven't been," she said, with a nod.

"I'll need the names of everybody who hasn't been."

"What will you do?" she asked. "Threaten them?"

"Of course not," he said, giving her a bland stare. "Obviously we need to do something. And they need to know that you're not alone."

"What? Will you pull that big macho man thing on me?"

"You want me to?" he asked instantly.

She burst out laughing. "No, I sure don't," she said. "I'm pretty used to handling things myself."

"We all need help sometimes," he said, "even Levi and me."

She tilted her head to the side. "Do you now?"

"Of course."

"In what way?"

He instantly said, "Well, I've got two kids coming for the summer, and they'll be at my place in about three weeks. I haven't got a clue what to do with them." He studied her for a long moment, but her gaze was steady, right back at him. He really liked that. As a matter of fact, he was liking a whole lot about her. Damn Levi for even bringing up that angle.

"Kids can be fun," she said quietly. "Are they yours?"

He nodded. "A boy and a girl." And he mentioned their ages. "But that's not today's issue."

"Maybe it is," she said suddenly. "I don't want any innocent children brought into this."

"Well, we'll have it well handled before that time," he said, "and I have a place close to Levi, where I would take them to anyway."

"Good enough." she said. "But if anybody knows about them, chances are they could still be used as pawns."

He had to respect that she was concerned about his children—or any children caught up in this nightmare for that matter. "Thank you for thinking of them," he said. "I'm sure they'll be safe enough. We just need to get this dealt with and fast."

"Nothing's ever fast," she said. "These two have tentacles that seem to be really far-reaching."

"Maybe, but that doesn't mean, when something happens to them, and they're made an example of, the rest of the family won't cut their losses. They're only popular while they're making money for the family."

"That's true enough," she muttered. "They also don't have any children of their own."

"That's a good thing," he said. "Then we won't be leaving any children fatherless." His hard tone left absolutely nothing for her to misunderstand.

"Are you really planning on killing them?"

He gave her a flat stare. "No," he said, frowning. "Absolutely not. I'm not planning anything. Yet. But, believe me, if they're looking to pressure me, threaten me, or take out any more old folks who happen to own property, that's something they'll have to go through me for."

"I don't imagine very much gets through you," she said, with a laugh.

"Not in a very long time," he said, with a smile. "But then my size can be a bit of a deterrent."

"You think?" she said. "I'm six foot. How tall are you?"

"Six-seven," he said, with a broad smile.

She smiled. "Not too many guys your height around here."

"Nope," he said, "you could even wear heels, and I'd still tower over you."

She laughed at that. "I love to wear heels on a date," she said. "But my dates don't usually like it because it puts me over their heads."

"Just guys who are insecure," he said comfortably.

She smiled. "And that's not you, is it?"

"Nope," he said. "I had one marriage that was great, until it wasn't, and it took me a long time to work off the anger and frustration I was left with. I don't necessarily consider myself a prize, just a good person who, as Levi would say, always tries to land on the side of right."

"And that's pretty hard to argue with," she said, as she smiled. "But back to this. I'm not exactly sure what you can do for a week or two. I was just hoping for a bit of backup to see how we can get through this."

"But do you have some deadline here?" he asked.

She looked at him in surprise. "What do you mean?"

"Well, you said for a week or two."

"Right, and of course you have other things you need to do too, right?"

He frowned. "That's not why I'm asking," he said. "I won't leave to go off and do something else without taking care of your problem here. I'm just trying to see if some deadline is involved, from the bad guys' perspective or yours. Do you have any reason to think you'll see an end to this in the next week or two?" He watched as she frowned, looked down at her papers, and shuffled them around aimlessly.

"No," she said, finally looking up. "I don't have an end plan because I don't really have a game plan at all."

"Well, first let's gather information."

"Okay, what information would you like?" she asked, with a ghost of a smile.

"Have you done any tracking on their bank accounts?"

One eyebrow twitched, and she smiled. "A little," she said. "I'm not as tech-savvy as a lot of Levi's crew, but I haven't been in this job without learning something."

"Can I?"

"Can you what?"

"Take that part over?"

"If you know how, then please, yes, jump right in."

"Let's track down the bank accounts first," he said, "and tax records, although legally we'd need something to drive that investigation—although it might be better to get Levi to look into that. We'll take a peek at what we might be looking at and do a full run on their banking. If we can get the feds involved," he said, "that'll change things entirely."

She settled back and said, "What do you need to do in

order to dig out that information?"

He gave her a ghost of a smile. "Well, if I don't have to tell you, then you can't be held liable later."

She rolled her eyes. "Is it legal? Will it stand up in court?"

"If Levi or I find something," he said, "then we can track down proof that *will* stand up in court."

She nodded slowly. "I guess I don't have much choice really, do I?"

"Not a lot, no," he said. "But, first, I want you to take a ride with me and show me where these properties are. I'll have a better feel of the area, once I actually see it."

She looked at him in surprise but willingly stood up. "Okay. Most of them are scattered about. But the two deaths that hold the most promise for pinning this on these brothers involves three tracts that connect. Still, I don't know what that'll show you," she said slowly.

"It'll tell me a lot about who they are," he said. "Come on. It will do you some good to get out of here."

"That's true," she said, with a wistful smile. She walked out to the front and said, "Lana, we're heading out for a drive. I'll be back in a little bit."

The friendly receptionist looked up, smiled, and nodded.

As they walked out, he said, "Does Lana do much to lighten your load?"

Immediately Angela shook her head. "Nope, she doesn't. But she's almost as iconic at the place as I am."

"In other words, she's part of the status quo, and you don't mess with it."

"Yep," she said. "She greets the people, handles the routine administrative tasks, the phones, the mail, some filing, simple stuff like that."

"Well, we all need that too," he said. He unlocked the truck and opened up the passenger door for her, then walked around to the driver's side. When she still hadn't gotten in, he looked over the roof at her and asked, "What's wrong? What's the matter?"

She gave a headshake, hopped in, and slammed the door shut.

He got in himself and looked at her. "Did I do something wrong?"

"No," she said, but a puzzled note was in her voice.

"That no sounded an awful lot like a yes."

"I just wasn't expecting the southern courtesy."

"The door, you mean?" She nodded. He shrugged. "You still have to be who you are, even in the midst of adversity," he said. "I will always open a door for a lady."

She burst out laughing. "It's been a hell of a long time since anybody saw me as a lady."

"It doesn't matter what shield you wear on your shoulders," he said. "You're still female at heart."

She smiled. "Thank you."

He turned on the engine, backed out of the parking lot, and asked, "Which way?"

"Take a left," she said and watched as he expertly maneuvered the big truck onto the road.

"Well, for better or for worse," he said, "here we go."

"I'm not sure what you mean by that, but it doesn't sound exactly how I expect this to go."

"Not to worry," he said, with a laugh. "We've got this."

Chapter 2

ANGELA WATCHED AS Bonaparte followed her directions to the location of the first property. As they drove slowly past the huge wrought iron gates, she looked at it and frowned.

"What's the frown about?"

"Wondering what the heavy security is for," she countered. She studied the gate and realized that it had been boosted since she had seen it last. "That fencing and gate wasn't quite this substantial before," she said.

"They're gaining enemies," he said, "and they're aware of it."

"Doesn't make a lot of difference," she said. "Enemies come and go, but these guys seem to keep winning."

"Maybe, maybe not," he said. He drove past, hoping to go around the block but realized that they had quite a large acreage. "Do you have any details on what they own?"

"Just basic data," she said. "It's a twenty-acre parcel."

"What are they doing with the twenty acres?"

"I don't know," she said. "I don't have any right to pry. All I have here is public information."

He snorted at that. "When people are after you," he said, "you have the right to do anything you need to do in order to make sure you're safe."

"Well, I wasn't really thinking of it in that way," she

said.

"That's because you were being defensive and not offensive," he said. "It's well past time to get offensive."

She frowned but had to agree that he was correct. She just hadn't seen it. She had been so busy trying to protect her staff and everybody else, while figuring out what she could do, that she hadn't actually decided to step ahead and do it. "I get that," she said, "but what difference does it make what they have for property?"

"It depends on if they're doing something illegal with it," he said. "Remember. We want to get as much intel as we can. We don't want to take them down for something minor. We want to take them down for something major."

"Is murder not major enough?" she asked.

"Absolutely," he said, "that's as big as it gets. But you also know that sentences and proof can vary a lot."

"Too much," she said. "I'd just as soon have them disappear forever, but I don't want us to put that out there."

"No, but, if we can get the brothers for money laundering, which is likely if their father is part of the crime family," he said, "that's a whole different story."

"And how will we find evidence of that?" she said.

"Well, let's figure out what their income is, let's figure out what they spend their money on, and put a case together."

"I was focused on the properties they bought. I wasn't thinking of the whole money angle."

"It's always about money," he said quietly.

"Unless it's about power," she said.

He laughed. "And that's usually about money too."

"And what about jealousy and rage?"

"I'll give you that one," he said. "When it comes to love

gone wrong, it becomes something else entirely. It's still a power trip, taking control away from somebody though."

"I guess. It's hard to look at our fellow man that way. I went into law enforcement because I wanted to help."

"You still want to help," he said, with a smile. "But don't worry about it too much. People are still just people."

"Always, it's just that now we've got a couple really ugly assholes in town."

"That happens to be my specialty," he said cheerfully.

She laughed and genuinely relaxed a moment. "In that case, I'm glad Levi sent you."

He looked over at her, smiled, and said, "You don't know the half of it."

She grinned. "Now, if you carry on," she said, "in another mile, you'll see the second property."

"Are they that close together?"

"Yes," she said.

"Do the two guys actually live in the residences?"

"Well, I thought so, but I haven't seen them around in quite a while."

"Besides," he said, "what is here for them? That's what I don't understand."

"I don't know that either. They said they just needed a place to get away from it all."

"Sure, and I can see that to a certain extent, but I just wonder if they were seeking something in particular about the location here."

"Well, it's five to ten minutes out of town, so, in a way, it's perfect for a lot of people." He nodded, giving her that point. She smiled. "Even though this isn't necessarily where a lot of people would like to live, it is a perfect choice for others."

"What are property prices doing?"

"They're shooting up."

"So, if they did nothing but buy up all the properties and wait for the prices to go up, they'd still make a killing."

"Yes. Absolutely."

"So another reason for doing what they're doing."

"But it's hardly fair," she said.

"These guys don't care about fair."

"No, that's true." He just kept on driving. Finally she said, "Up ahead is the next property." It was on the same side of the road, and, as he got up there, another large gate was here, almost identical to the one they had seen already on the other property.

"Do they keep animals?"

"Again, I don't know," she said. "We have no registry, unless it's a large commercial operation."

"Right," he said. He drove around for a little bit, then veered off on the roadside, pulled up his laptop, while she watched.

"What are you doing?"

"Just bringing up the satellite, so I can take a look at these properties." And then he sent a message to Levi, explaining where he was and requesting one of his team look into the bank records and the tax returns on the two brothers. "Levi said you're supposed to update him," he said, after the laptop beeped.

She snorted. "I figured you'd be doing that."

"Yep, I'll do it on a regular basis."

"He's a good guy," she said suddenly.

"One of the best," Bonaparte said, without even lifting his gaze from the laptop screen.

She studied his intensity. "I don't understand this.

Where are you getting the satellite feed from?"

He looked up at her, smiled, and said, "Levi."

Her eyebrows shot up. "Oh. I don't think I knew he had that."

"Yeah. An agreement within an agreement within an agreement," he said. "But it's been invaluable for a lot of the cases Levi works on."

"Is it giving us anything?"

"A lot of buildings on this property make no sense to me," he said. "And they're big. What was here before they bought it?"

She thought about it and said, "A whiskey distillery." He looked at her in surprise. She smiled and said, "It didn't do very well."

"But that would explain the buildings."

"That's what I thought," she said. "Some of them. Are they setting up shop? They haven't applied for a license, as far as I'm aware."

"I don't know. I have no idea what they're up to. Maybe nothing. For all we know, they looked at these two proper-ties, wanting to have places near each other and within driving distance to town, and these are the ones they bought." He paused. "Was there anything funny about them when they bought them?"

"Not that I know of," she said. "I didn't hear about any-thing being off."

"Was it a clean sale? And, if you tell me again you don't know, then we'll go find the old owners."

"You can't," she said suddenly.

"Why is that?" he said, shooting her a look.

She frowned. "Because they're two of the dead."

He settled back.

"Okay, so this is a little unnerving. Are these guys just killing people outright?"

"Well, it was a car accident," she said. "We did investigate it, but the road conditions were nasty, and the car went over the edge of one of the highways here. It was actually quite a job to retrieve the bodies and to clear out the wreck."

"And there was nothing foul about it?"

"At the time, I agreed with the coroner that it was accidental. But, as things started to stack up, I began to get suspicious."

"A pretty convenient accident," he said. "But it doesn't seem like anything with these guys is accidental at all."

"There's no need for them to kill people," she said. "These owners probably, eventually would have sold without a problem."

"So, if the owners died, who would these assholes have bought these properties from?"

"I think one went to a cousin in New York, when the estate was settled. Then they approached him with a price and bought it."

"Do you think he would have sold anyway?"

"No, the cousin was planning on moving here and getting the distillery back up and running," she said quietly. She stared out the window, hating the thought that she might not have done her due diligence and might have missed something. "I'll feel really shitty," she said, "if it turns out they really were murdered."

"What about this property here?"

"I understand they had gotten offers but, over the years, were never interested. However, with family health issues and property prices going straight up more recently, I understand he was more interested lately."

"Well, let's look into that one too," he said.

"But still, the thing is, these guys have money," she said in exasperation. "There was no need to kill anybody, unless the owner was adamant, and he didn't want to sell. See? When all this was going on, it wasn't on my radar. Only after people started dying did it all start to smell bad."

"We do have wealthy people out there in this world who just want a property because they can't have it. Maybe it was worth it to them. Maybe this is all some game," he said.

"A game to kill people?"

"I've seen it happen time and time again," he said. "Nothing is nice or easy about any of it, but it does happen."

She shook her head. "Now that you mention the money issue, I would say something much more businesslike is about it."

"Meaning?"

"If they bought the properties, it was likely for some reason that we don't understand yet. And it'll all be about money."

"Is that all they are?"

"Yes," she said, "you're so right. They're all about money. And showing it off."

"Interesting. Do they have wives or partners of some sort?"

"No, they have decorations."

He stared at her blankly for a moment and then started to laugh. "Okay, I get the idea. You feel fairly strongly about it too."

"They come from the big city, and they are rich high-rollers, who cause chaos wherever they go. They go to the coffee shop or the bar, have absolutely nothing nice to say about any of it, throw enough money around to keep people happy and accepting of their ignorant behavior, and then they're gone."

"Well, there are more than a few towns with assholes like that," he murmured.

"Yeah, but our town used to be nice. We didn't have people like that."

"Sorry," he said. "When those types move in, they're quite the pain in the ass."

She snorted. "In this case they are claiming our town as home, if that's what you call it, but that still doesn't make it illegal, and absolutely nothing here proves that they did anything wrong."

"Nope. I want to see the accident report on the guy who owned this property, and we'll do an investigation into the other one to make sure it was aboveboard."

"How will you do that?"

"I want to talk to the other owner."

"Jeremy is in old folks home, and his daughter sold it."

"Good, let's go talk to her." She hesitated. He looked at her and asked, "Is that a problem?"

She sighed. "No, let's go do it."

He nodded and asked, "Which way?"

She gave him directions to her best friend's house.

BONAPARTE WASN'T SURE what Angela's reaction meant. "Is there a problem here that I need to be aware of?"

"No," she said. "Gladys is the woman who sold the property for her father. Her daughter is a good friend of mine, that's all."

"And this is a conflict of interest?"

"When you're the sheriff of a small town like this, all of

it is a conflict of interest," she said, with a quirk of her lips.

He thought about it and nodded. "I guess it does make things awkward at various times, doesn't it?"

"It does, but I've been in this job for a few years," she said. "I'll make it through a few more too. At least if we can deal with the interference from these assholes."

"Good enough," he said. She directed him toward town and then to a right turn, where they veered off to another corner. "This is an interesting area," he said.

"Yes."

"So, what is it we're looking for here?"

She pointed out the address as they got closer. "That little brownstone over there," she said. "That's Isabel's place."

"Got it," he said, and he pulled up in the front. Almost immediately the front door opened, and Isabel stepped out, a frown on her face. But, when she saw Angela hop from the truck, a smile lit up her features.

"Hey," she said. "What's with the truck?" And when Bonaparte got out, her eyes widened. "What's with the mammoth?"

"This is Bonaparte," Angela said. "He's one of the deputies who'll be working with me." The words seemed to roll off her lips quite easily.

Bonaparte reached out a hand to shake Isabel's and smiled. "Hey, nice to meet you."

"Good Lord," she said. "We don't see too many people your size around here," her gaze going from Bonaparte to Angela and back again.

"Nope," he said, "not too many anywhere."

At that, she looked startled, and then she laughed. "Isn't that the truth? I'm sorry. I'm being rude. Come on in."

"I just need to ask you a few questions," Angela said.

Isabel stopped in her tracks, looked at her, and said, "Are these difficult questions?"

"I don't think so," she said, "but I don't know. When your mother sold your grandfather's property up on Alston Way?"

Isabel nodded.

"Were there any issues with the sale?"

An odd look came on Isabel's face. "What do you mean by *issues?*"

She shrugged. "Obviously there was something because now you are prevaricating."

Isabel rolled her eyes. "You can't use big words on me and expect me to know what they mean."

Angela sighed. "I'm not using big words. I just asked you a question, but, instead of answering me, you got this nervous look."

"Well, there was something. We had two buyers. Remember?"

"I remember you telling me that there were two bidders. I presumed you took the largest and walked."

"Well, we did, and we didn't," she said. "We wanted to sell it locally. Remember James? He died in the car accident ..."

"Another car accident?" Bonaparte asked Angela, who nodded.

Isabel continued, "I mean, it's a good thing that we didn't sell it to him after all," she said, "but he was pretty upset when we wouldn't. He wanted to keep it local, and we actually ended up selling it to the rich guy from out of town."

"And was there any pressure to sell to him?" Bonaparte

asked, watching Isabel's face, and caught that slight conster-nation. "So there was. What kind of pressure?"

She frowned, her lips thinning, as she looked from one to the other.

"Is there a problem?" Bonaparte asked.

"We need to know the extent of the pressure this guy has put on locals," Angela said.

"Well, it wasn't really pressure. I mean, how much pres-sure can it be? He paid good money for the property. We needed to sell, as you know."

"I know," she said quietly. "But was your mother put under any undue pressure? Why would you choose him over James?"

"It was Mom, I think, as much as anything," she said. "I didn't care who bought it, but James died in a car accident, and the other guy? I don't even remember his name," she said, almost nervously looking around, as they stood outside on her front walk. "He went through with the sale, so we were happy, and we got our money, and it was done." She put up her hands in a gesture of a *what can you do* motion and added, "We were just happy to have it over with."

Bonaparte pressed the point. "And why is that?"

Isabel looked at him and then at Angela. "Why the inter-rogation?"

"Well, it would help if you would just answer our ques-tions," Angela said. "We're trying to figure out if there's been any wrongdoing by this buyer."

She frowned at that. "Well, he's one scary dude," she said. "But Mom up and sold and was quite happy to."

"Of course. Did she receive any threats, telling her to sell or suggesting what would happen if she didn't?"

"Oh, ouch," she said. "Yeah, there was. I mean, I happily

forgot about it for a long time." She sighed. "And I really don't like you bringing it up either," she said, her tone turning cross. "We have enough problems."

"And what problems are those?" Bonaparte asked. Angela looked like she would answer, but he gave a slight headshake. Instead, Isabel looked at him and said, "Just that my granddad's in the old folks' home. And he's causing quite the kerfuffle there."

"And your mom?"

"She doesn't have great health either," Isabel said, then shrugged. "We did what we had to do to take care of them both."

"Do you mind telling us all the details then?" Angela said quietly. "You're not in trouble. But we need to know what we're facing with the guy who bought it."

A look of almost fear crossed her face. She looked behind Bonaparte and said, "I don't know." She shook her head. "It's not the same town it used to be."

"No, it isn't," Angela said. "And I'm trying to make it that way again."

"I don't know that you can," she said. "It's not, ... well, as long as these guys are around, it's not the same."

"Have they ever contacted you since?"

She shook her head. "No, not really."

"Not really?" Bonaparte pressed.

She shrugged and glared at him. "You don't have to be so accusingly about it."

"I need to know exactly what happened," he said, "and so does Angela."

She groaned. "Fine. Every once in a while, they drive by really slow out front."

"As in a threatening manner?" he asked.

"I don't know that it's a threatening manner, as much as I don't know that it isn't," she said. "But it does what it's intended to do. It made me scared, keeps me scared."

"But did you do anything wrong?"

"They said we did," she said in a low whisper. She looked around the block and then said, "You'd better come on inside." She opened the door wider, and they walked inside.

And as soon as they got in, he leaned against the closed door and said, "What did you do wrong?"

She looked at Angela, and then, with shame in her eyes, she said, "We forged granddad's signature on the sale form."

Angela closed her eyes and sighed. "You didn't have power of attorney, did you?"

"No, he never would give it to us," she said. "But you know that's what he wanted to happen. And what we had to have happen."

"Jesus. And they found out?" Angela asked.

"Yeah, but I don't know how," Isabel said. "That's the thing that I can't figure out."

"But, in the meantime, they're using fear to keep you in line," Bonaparte noted. "Or just on the hook."

"I know. The thing is, I mean, we needed to sell. It wouldn't do any harm to sell to him, so it's not like we were doing anything wrong there. Granddad was there, but we just helped him to make that signature happen," she said, with a shrug.

"So you held his hand and signed it for him?" Angela asked.

"Yes." She shrugged. "Was it wrong? Maybe. We didn't know what else to do. We actually had a buyer. Granddad had been trying to sell for years anyway, as you well know," she said in exasperation.

Angela turned to look at her friend. "Sure, but there's legal, and then there's not legal."

"Well, I don't know what we're supposed to do if that was not legal," she said. "But obviously it wasn't because they keep driving by. Yet they got the property, so why do they care?"

"How often?" Bonaparte had a good idea why, but he kept it to himself. Angela would get it; her friend, well, she hadn't yet.

"I don't think it's that often anymore," she said, "but every once in a while. It's just enough. And because I'm always looking for them now, it's kind of hard because you expect to see them out of the corner of your eye all the time, so it makes you jumpy."

"What it does," he said, "is make you look over your shoulder for the rest of your life."

Her shoulders sagged. "I know," she said, "but that's what we did, and I don't know what I am supposed to do about it."

"And was it in your granddad's name, free and clear?" Bonaparte asked.

"Yes," she said, "and there's only my mother. It's in the will that she's supposed to get it, and we needed the money for his care. He'd been trying to sell it for months and months beforehand."

He thought about it and nodded. "So, in many ways, you just jumped the gun a little bit."

"In many ways," she said, "we were trying to play catch-up. Because he was trying to sell anyway. If this had happened just a little bit earlier, it wouldn't have mattered, but granddad's not quite himself anymore. But he does have lucid days."

"And that would be your argument, right?" Angela asked. "If anybody questioned it, it was on one of his lucid days."

She nodded slowly. "And remember at that time we didn't know how bad his mental state was failing. He had many lucid days," she said, "but he wasn't really capable of signing very well, so we just helped him."

"And did you talk to him about it?"

"Yes, and he was excited."

"So why did you feel like it was illegal?"

"Because he was only lucid for a little bit," she said, "and we didn't get the signatures done in time, so we had to give him a little help. So, of course, we felt guilty," she said, "because it wasn't quite kosher. But really it was."

And then Angela just nodded, as if she weren't quite sure what to think about it. And Bonaparte understood. These things were delicate at the best of times. And was there ever a clear-cut case in an instance like this? "Anybody else see you or know about it?"

"We didn't think so," she said. "We were alone in Granddad's room in the nursing home, so either the buyer guessed, or we let on, or we somehow ... I don't know," she said in exasperation. "I really don't know."

"How long ago was the sale?"

"About four months," she said.

"And what did you do with the money?"

"It's in the bank, paying for my mom's cancer treatments and Granddad's care."

"Right," Bonaparte said. "So, even if he were cognizant and aware, he would have been okay with that, right?"

"Exactly," she said with relief. "It's exactly what he

would have wanted. We were all very close, weren't we?" She turned to face Angela, who nodded slowly.

"Yes," Angela said. "If he were cognizant, he would have definitely signed to help get the money to help your mom. And, like you said, it was for sale for months."

"Why do you think nobody would buy it?" Bonaparte immediately interrupted.

"I suspect," Isabel said, "the price we were asking was just too high."

"That's possible. And this guy paid full price?"

She winced. "No. It started off that way, but then, before we got to the end of the purchase, he had been dropping the offer. By the time we got to closing the deal, it was quite a bit less than if we had sold to James. So that was something that made us really angry, but, because he more or less had us behind the eight ball, there wasn't anything we could do about it."

"Which is why they did it that way," he said, with a nod. "Okay, you need to let us know the next time you feel scared or see that vehicle drive slowly by. What kind of vehicle was it?"

"He's got a muscle car," she said. "You know? One of those things with that raised piece in the front that sounds really loud and dangerous."

He nodded. "Black, I presume?"

She snorted. "Of course, shiny with lots of chrome. How did you know?"

He shrugged and said, "It's fairly typical."

"Wow, so anytime I see one of those vehicles when I'm in the city, I'll think they're all assholes."

"No, that's not quite fair," he said, with a smile. "But you'd be amazed at how many of these guys drive vehicles like that because they think it makes them look dangerous."

"Well, these guys are dangerous," she said suddenly. "He didn't come right out and say that we would pay, but it was implied that, if we told anybody about the pressure they'd put on us …" And then she stopped and said, "You know what? It wasn't even that. It was all just impressions. It was all just that sense that we were in deep trouble and that they knew something about us and that we would go to jail for it. They didn't really do anything wrong, but then neither did we. It's like the whole deal was in the shadows. I couldn't believe just how grateful I was when it was done, and they actually paid."

"Well, they have lots of money," Angela said, "so it makes sense that they would pay. If nothing else it gives them more power again for having done so."

Isabel shrugged. "I don't get how any of that works," she said, with a shiver. "We're just simple folk here."

"Simple folk maybe," Bonaparte said quietly, "but that doesn't mean you're stupid. You knew exactly what was going on. Otherwise you wouldn't feel guilty now, and they wouldn't have been able to pressure you into it being afraid every time you see them."

"Right," she said, "well, I'm wholeheartedly admitting to knowing about it."

"And you don't have any compunction about your granddad having a problem with it?"

"No," she said. "When we told him that we had a buyer, he was over the moon. He'd been really worried about Mom's care. He wanted to sell right away."

"Good enough," he said. He turned to look at Angela. "Anywhere else you want to go?"

She turned and looked at her friend, gave her a hug, and

said, "We'll talk later." Then she walked out. As they got back to the truck, she asked, "Do you believe her?"

He looked at her sharply. "You don't?"

"I do," she said, "but something was in her tone."

"Outside of the fact that she's afraid she'll get thrown in jail or the fact that she'll lose her friend, who is even now looking at her as if she might be a criminal?"

She nodded. "Yeah, I guess that's a big part of it, isn't it?"

"Whenever somebody fesses up to a crime like that," he said, "even if it feels justified at the time, they know it's wrong, so they're always looking over their shoulders. And some guys like this, they're just predators. Predators in the business world," he said. "They could have made them do anything. It wouldn't even have taken much. Even now that leverage is a perfect blackmail tool."

"Sounds like they did," she said, with a heavy heart. "Now Isabel's always got that fear going on."

"Absolutely," he said, "and that'll make it tougher for her as well."

"She's a really nice person," she said, "and everything she's doing would be entirely to save her mom."

"I get it," he said. "Really. Don't worry. I do get it."

She smiled, nodded, and said, "I'm glad. Because she's good people."

"Isabel might be, but even good people do wrong."

Angela groaned. "I know. I know. I know."

And, with that, he had to be satisfied.

Chapter 3

"**N**OW WHERE?" ANGELA asked, as he drove the truck back the way they had come.

Bonaparte looked at the clock on the dashboard and said, "I'm hungry."

"And where will you stay?" she asked, with a tilt to her lips.

"I'm staying at your place," he said immediately.

She stared at him in shock. "You don't even wait for an invitation?" she asked in a droll tone.

"Nope," he said, "too many undercurrents going on here. The sooner they figure out where I'm staying, the better, and then we can assess your property too, from a defensive standpoint."

"Sometimes I think I'm making too big of a deal out of this."

"You're not," he replied.

"But you don't know that for sure," she said. He looked over at her, and she went quiet. "Okay, I wish I'd known about what had happened to Isabel."

"She couldn't tell you. She didn't dare tell you," he said, "because, even now, she's afraid you'll arrest her."

"And yet, in theory, if it was her mom's idea, it's her mom who should be arrested."

"Sure, except that she also hid the truth from you."

"I know. But there wasn't an investigation, so it's not like she lied to me."

"Nope, so she's free and clear."

She sighed. "It still feels odd."

"The joys of being in law enforcement and having a lot of friends you care about, and, in this case, they were pressured to do something because of the circumstances, so you'll have to figure out how you feel about it."

"But this is where *right* becomes cloudy."

"Nope, not at all," he said. "You just have to sit down and think it through. And, if you need to talk to somebody, there are people you can talk to."

"Yes," she said, "I do have someone. I can talk to the prosecutor."

"I can tell you that he'll say there's no case."

"Which would be fine because, if I know that ahead of time," she said, "I don't have to feel guilty about it."

He smiled. "And you can let Isabel know that she's off the hook."

"Right," she said, with a sigh, "because that is something she won't rest about now, will she?"

"Would you?"

"No," she said, with a laugh. "I wouldn't."

"See? So it's pretty easy to figure out."

"Right and wrong is not always that clear," she said.

"No, sometimes it takes a little bit to work your way through, but it becomes clear eventually. So, where to?"

She looked at him in confusion.

"Do you have groceries?" he asked. "Or do we need to go out for dinner or stop at the store?"

She laughed. "So now you're inviting yourself for dinner too."

"Well, I figured, if I offered to take you out for dinner, you'd likely get mad at me."

"Why would I do that?" she asked in astonishment.

"Well, opening the door was a strange thing for you. You are an officer of the law, so I don't want to make it sound like I'm compelling you to do something or that I'm disrespecting your office," he said, with a knowing smile. "But I'd really like to take you out for a good steak."

Her eyes widened. "A good steak would be perfect," she said. "I'll take you up on that offer."

"So where am I headed then?" he asked.

She smiled and said, "Away from here and back into town."

"If you say so," he said. "Is it nice and public?"

"Yes, of course it is," she said, frowning. "Why wouldn't it be?"

"Nothing," he said. "I just want to make sure it's really public."

She groaned. "You want to make sure everybody thinks that the pretty little sheriff has a partner, is that it?"

"No, not at all," he said. "I want everybody to know that the sheriff has a *deputy*," he said. "One who's not afraid to back his boss up."

She looked at him, smiled, and said, "You know what? That just might work."

"Doesn't matter if you're female or not, by the way," he said. "I'd step up for the side of right any time, any day, any place, anyhow."

She chuckled. "There's a lot to be said for that."

"There is," he said. "It makes it all nice and clear. So where's the steakhouse because I'm getting really hungry now."

Still laughing, she directed him to the one on Main Street. "That should be public enough for you," she said.

"Good," he said. "Let everybody know, right off the bat, that you are no longer alone and that somebody around here has your back."

"I can get behind that," she said quietly, as he parked the truck. She looked around and smiled because, even now, people were studying the strange truck. "Don't look now," she said, "but we're already attracting attention."

"Good. The more, the better."

BONAPARTE PARKED, SHUT off the engine, then looked at Angela and grinned. "Let's go, boss."

Still laughing, she hopped out and led the way to the front of the restaurant. She didn't even think about it, but he was that half step ahead of her and pulled open the door.

"Will you do that all the time? That'll take a lot out of you after a while."

"Takes nothing out of me to be nice or gentlemanly or polite," he said. "My mother raised me with manners, and I certainly don't intend to lose them just because I'm ready to take on the world."

She stepped in front of him and sighed happily at the cool air-conditioning that wafted toward her. "You don't realize how hot it is," she murmured, "until you step inside."

"That's when you realize just how much people are dependent on AC," he said. "Nothing wrong with a good hot day."

"Well, there's hot, and then there's hot-hot," she said. "I'm okay with hot, but I really don't like superhot."

"I'm with you there," he said. "Do you have any decent

creeks around this place for swimming?"

"There's a couple," she said in surprise, looking at him. "And I do have a pool at my place." At that, his eyes widened in joy. He grinned at her. "All the more reason."

"Good evening, Sheriff," one of the young waitresses said, as she walked toward them. "Are you here for dinner?"

"Yes," she said. "I'm taking my new deputy out for his first meal here in town," she said smoothly.

He had to laugh at her maneuvering because essentially she had just said that he couldn't pay for her dinner either. Still chuckling to himself, he followed her and the waitress to a booth in the center of the restaurant. It was an interesting location because it put them right in the hot seat. But he knew they had everybody's attention regardless.

He was more or less used to getting attention wherever he went because of his size, and he imagined she was too, but together they made quite a sight. He was all for it. The problem with dating tiny women was that it always felt like they were little china dolls, and he could break them. Now this one, Angela, she looked like somebody who could hold her own. Of course they were garnering quite a bit of attention.

He let his gaze move around the room, slowly and carefully, noting the various levels of attention and opinionated looks they were getting. A couple on the side immediately looked away when Bonaparte caught their gaze. Several suited men looked like they were having a business dinner, yet they were more interested and curious than most in the restaurant. Bonaparte's gaze next landed on two local guys, both wearing hats, who would never be welcome in terms of any big city restaurant. And they were hiding behind them at the same time. He noted their other features to ask Angela about when they got a moment. At another booth farther down, somebody sat aloof and alone. And yet the waitresses were running around him, as if he were somebody.

As soon as they were seated, and Angela had smiled and thanked the waitress, Angela then said, "Holly, could you bring coffee right away, please?"

Holly just smiled and said, "Sure thing," and she took off. Bonaparte pointed out the ones he had noticed in particular. She nodded and said, "The two men in the hats are Leroy and Leonard."

"Isn't that cliché?" he said.

"Their mama would never let them come in here with a hat on, so, the minute she was dead, they refused to take them off," she said. "In all fairness, they aren't 100 percent all there mentally. They have some disability, but I don't know that she ever got them tested."

He nodded. "So, in other words, we're just dealing with teenage rebellion in adult bodies."

"In forty-year-old men, yeah," she said, with an understanding smile.

"And the other one?" he asked, nodding to the man at the back.

She twisted and took one look, slowly reversing, until she faced Bonaparte again. In a lowered voice, she said, "That's Ronnie, one of our troublemakers. His brother is Johnny."

Bonaparte looked at her in surprise and studied the man. "He's older than I thought."

"He looks older, yes," she said. "My understanding is that he's just turned thirty-eight."

"Interesting. I was thinking early thirties," he murmured. It was hard to get a fix on him, but the way everybody was acting said a lot. "He really thinks he's somebody, doesn't he?"

"News flash," she said, her lips twitching. "He is somebody."

"So are we," he said.

"Hey, I got some service when I walked in," she said. "I wasn't sure I'd even get that."

He looked at her in surprise. "Would they be so blatant?"

"It's hard to say," she said. "Just when you think you know what's going on around here, you don't."

"Understood," he murmured. He picked up the menu in front of him and asked, "What's good?"

"Pretty much everything," she said, "but I really like the ribs."

"Ribs are good," he said, with a nod. "Steak is what I'm after."

"So is the steak," she said.

By the time Holly came back with the coffee, they were ready with their order. Holly wrote it down quickly and left.

"She looks like she's in a hurry."

"Whether that's because it's busy," Angela said, "or because her bosses rattled her about us, I don't know."

"You wouldn't expect it to be quite so overt," he murmured.

"I know. It's been getting worse over time," she said, her voice equally quiet. "And I can't blame them. Everybody is rattled and wondering where things will go from here."

"Of course," he murmured. "There's that sense of waiting, isn't there?"

"Yes, there is, and it's pretty unnerving."

"Does it bother you?"

"Well, it's like when the weather is building up, and you know it's about to break, but it hasn't yet, so you're hot and muggy and feeling sticky and just wishing it would happen, so you could get on with life."

"Right, but these kinds of storms have a tendency to not be something that you actually get over," he murmured. They kept their conversation low, as they discussed various people who had interested him in the room. They were still the center of attention, as everybody turned to look and then would look away, as soon as he caught their gaze.

"But nobody is being overtly unfriendly," he said, "nor have they been overtly friendly."

"No," she said, "it's just that strange weightiness." Even as they waited for their meals to arrive, several people got up, as if hurriedly finishing to leave.

"Was that because of us?"

"It's possible," she said, slowly studying the room and its occupants. "I haven't really had them get up and leave when I'm here yet, but—because you're here and an unknown, and of course Ronnie is here—maybe this combo has them jumpy."

"You think that's what it is?"

"I wouldn't put it past anybody," she said. "Most of the town is just sleepy, and people don't want to be bothered. They just want to go about their daily life without dealing with any of this strife. The fact that it's come home in a big way makes them uncomfortable. It makes them nervous, and they don't want anything to do with it." As they watched, another couple got up, leaving a little bit on their plates, and walked over to the cashier, where they paid hurriedly and walked out. She nodded and said, "Now they are definitely leaving because of the scenario."

"Good," he said. "When bullets fly, fewer people are here to catch a stray one."

"Well, bullets flying is one thing," she said, "but bullets flying inside a restaurant full of people is a whole different story."

He spied the waitress coming toward him just then. She carried large platters and looked to be in a hurry. "Here's dinner," he said, settling back, as a large platter was put in front of him and another before Angela, as Holly skittered off again. He looked at his food and smiled. "Maybe our money is just as good as everybody else's here because this looks lovely."

"Might be better than everybody else's, as the owner's an old friend," she said easily, "but that doesn't mean he can handle being too friendly with me."

Bonaparte didn't care how friendly the owner was as long as the steak tasted as good as it looked. He looked over at her ribs and nodded. "Those look damn fine too."

She gave him a fat grin. "They are," she said. "I wasn't kidding. It really is the best thing on the menu, if you ask me." She picked up her knife and fork and started separating the ribs. He could see the meat fall off the bone, as he looked down at his steak. His mouth started to water, and he cut in, anticipating that first bite. He had just lifted it and put it in his mouth, when a man interrupted them.

"So who the hell are you?"

Bonaparte looked up to see the arrogant asshole from the back booth standing in front of them. His hands on his hips, his legs planted wide apart, almost as if he were a cowboy, heading for a gunfight. Bonaparte smiled and said, "New deputy," mumbling around his mouthful of food.

"Yeah, she goes through them pretty fast, doesn't she?"

he said, as he eyed Bonaparte up and down. But a seated Bonaparte was still a hell of a lot taller than most people standing. Angela ignored Ronnie entirely and just continued to eat. "How can you possibly want to work for a woman?" he asked.

"Got no problem working for a woman," Bonaparte said. "That's the job."

"Yeah, but there are better jobs," he said. "This is just, you know, somebody who should be staying home with their kids. Oh, but wait, she doesn't have any." He gave a hard laugh. "She hasn't got a man either. Maybe that's what your deal is."

"I wouldn't say so," he said, "and it takes a lot for somebody to actually insult me like that."

"Insult intended," the guy said in a mocking tone. "Enjoy your dinner." He sneered as he looked at her, and then, with a wave of dismissal, he turned and walked to the front door. As soon as he stepped outside, a sense of peace was in the air, as everybody relaxed again.

"He really is an asshole, isn't he?" Bonaparte said, looking at Angela.

"He sure is," she muttered. "The thing is, I'm so used to him by now that I wouldn't ruin my ribs by even talking to him." She reached down, picked up one of the ribs with her fingers, and quickly slicked the bone clean. He had to laugh because he really appreciated somebody who chose enjoying good food over keeping her hands clean. He knew a lot of people who would have continued to eat the rib with a knife and fork, but then he'd also seen lots of people take a knife and fork to a good burger. And that was just sacrilegious. Bonaparte and Angela enjoyed the rest of their meal in relative peace. Holly came back and filled up their coffee, her smile even brighter.

When they were done, and Angela got up and walked over to pay, Bonaparte said, "You know that I can pay for my own."

"Yeah, I know," she said, "but I said I would do it, and I will."

He let her pay, noting that the bill was fairly reasonable, considering the amount of food they'd gotten.

As they stepped outside, she said, "So how was it under the microscope?"

"Interesting," he said; then he walked beside her and studied the area around them. "I'm used to it actually."

"I am too," she murmured.

He looked at her with a grin. "We're a matched set. Now lead the way home."

"Maybe," she said and then nodded toward the parking lot. "Except that we have company, and they've been watching us since we stepped out."

He nodded. "Yeah, I picked up on the four guys. Who are they?"

"Ronnie pays local kids to spy on various people," she murmured.

"That same guy who was in there?"

"Him and his brother, yes," she said. "It's a toss-up as to who it is at any given time."

"They just keeping feelers out or what?"

"I think so," she said. "It's hard to know just what they think they'll find out."

"I find this is all very fascinating. Like it's the next hot spot outside of Denver or something?"

"Well, there's definitely a lot suggesting that may be what they're working toward. They own a lot of land, and, if they could subdivide it and jump up the prices, or build condos and jump up the prices, they would make a killing."

"I suppose," he said. "You are close to Denver."

"We are," she said cheerfully. "We're also just far enough away that we're out of town. And we don't have to deal with the traffic or the smog it causes."

"So, in other words, it's almost perfect."

"Yes. Denver's within a forty-five-minute commute," she said, "and, for almost everybody, that's the sweet spot."

"So then, what the brothers are doing here makes sense from a property development point of view."

"Maybe so, and, from what Isabel said, the brothers offer a good sum at first, but bring the price down before closing, while running off any serious bidders, so they buy the property dirt cheap, regardless of the true property values," she said. "Manipulating, threatening, blackmailing—that's what they do to the property owners, just like what they did to my deputies. Maybe the brothers just sit here in town and work the angles until they make enough, and then they walk away to another unsuspecting town."

"It has to be enough of a profit to make it worthwhile," he said, "and I'm not sure this is."

"I think it probably is," she said. "The property prices here are really cheap when compared to Denver."

"Even cheaper if the bad guys are running off any other buyers, then harassing the sellers too."

Angela grimaced. "Figures. They are working both sides of the transaction, aren't they?"

"Are these guys doing the spying really young?" he asked. "As in teenagers?" He watched as the four spies walked away from them.

"Pretty much. Two are still in high school, as far as I

know. No truancy filings. The other two are dropouts, one was supposed to go to college and then couldn't get funding," she said quietly.

"So they're at loose ends?" Bonaparte asked.

"Not a whole lot of work in town," she said, "and Ronnie pays well."

"And I suppose these kids think of themselves as doing the world a service."

"I don't know about that, but they think it's cool, which makes them cool."

"Sure, they do," he said in disgust. "And he's preying on that sense of identity they're so desperate for."

"Of course," she said, with a smile. "Isn't that how we get everybody to do things they don't want to do?"

He shook his head and walked toward the parking lot, where they left the truck.

"And you'll talk to them?" she asked, rushing to keep up.

"Depends on if they talk to me first," he said casually. "I'm not looking for trouble, but it's there, if they want it."

"I think, between the two of us, we could take all four, don't you?"

"Hell, you're not allowed to cut in on my fun," he said. "I haven't had a good dustup in at least two days. All four are mine." She burst out laughing. Trouble was, he was serious. He looked over and saw that she knew it too.

She smiled, still chuckling. "You can see I'm used to Levi and his crew."

"It's a good thing you are too." They got to the parking lot to see that all the guys had scattered on foot in four different directions.

"Your size really does do that, doesn't it?" she murmured in surprise.

"First, I'm male," he said. "Second, I'm huge and I'm fit. I really don't like getting pushed around, and it probably shows," he said. "I can't stand sluggards and people being disrespectful. Most guys decide that it's just not worth the battle."

"I like that," she said. "Being tough doesn't really give me much of an edge."

"Basic genetics are against you in that field," he said. "Seriously I've known a lot of women who could handle a ton of shit, and they could take a lot of people, and you'd never know it at first glance. Like Kai, for example," he said. "She's at the top of the game, just like Ice. Generally they still get the same flak because they're attractive women."

"It's quite infuriating," Angela murmured.

"Unless you use it to your advantage. The guys never know what's coming, and that's something that Ice and Kai both play on. They know perfectly well that nobody expects what they can do, so, when it comes out of left field, these guys are trying to react, and they're already off their game, in which case, both Kai and Ice can move in for the kill."

"That's very true," she said, nodding.

"You just have to change your attitude about it all. Everything in life is attitude," he said. "You can't let all this get you down or influence your decision-making."

"It's not a case of getting me down," she said. "It's more about trying to figure out just what to do. I want this to stop now, and I want my town to go back to the way it was."

"So, using the view of hindsight," he said carefully, when they were both inside the truck, "can you actually look around this town and see that it ever really was the way you thought it was?"

She looked at him in surprise. "Ah," she said, "I see what

you're asking." She frowned, as she thought about it, and he respected her for at least considering his question. "I don't think I was ever oblivious to what was going on here," she said. "I did grow up here, so I've always known where the drugs are sold and where the alcohol is accessed by kids," she said. "I know a lot of those tiny dark corners of trouble and the people who cause it," she said, "but I've never ever known or seen evidence of anything like what's going on right now."

"Well, that's good," he said, "because, if it's new, as you believe, then it hasn't really had a chance to hide. These guys don't seem too bothered about hiding anyway. They must figure they have enough money to make everything go away."

"Well, they do," she said. "And sadly that's the problem. All of it is just going away."

"What's the worst thing that can happen here?" he asked.

"Well, they can buy up everything, turning it into a massive property development. There wouldn't be a sheriff since there won't be any need for it because it'll all be incorporated into the city itself, or they'll just install some security force of their own."

"Which is probably more likely because then they'll own the law too," he said.

"And that's what they're trying to do. Get rid of me, so they can put in their own people."

"You're in an elected position, right?"

"Yes," she said, "and I've already considered the fact that I may not get re-elected."

"It sounds almost likely, given the brothers' influence right now, doesn't it?"

"It does right now," she said, nodding sadly. "And, if this isn't what I'll do, I'll have to find another way to earn a living."

"That's always hard but not impossible."

She nodded, and then there wasn't a whole lot she could say.

He considered her for a moment, then started the engine and let it idle. "So tell me how to get to your place."

She smiled. "All of this on a first date?" she teased. "Who knew?"

"Levi knew." Bonaparte laughed.

Chapter 4

"**W**HAT ARE YOU talking about?" Angela asked in surprise. "What did Levi say?"

Bonaparte chuckled. "I wasn't even going to say anything, but his good old matchmaking heart is in full swing."

She groaned. "He's been at that for years," she said, with a heavy sigh. "He can't just see that I might be perfectly happy being single."

"In my experience, the happier married people are, the more they want the rest of the world around them to be happy too. The problem is, they think that you'll only be happy in the same marital state that they are in."

"Which, in this case, is permanently partnered," she said, with a nod.

"*Permanently partnered?*" He smiled, looking at her. "Huh. I haven't heard that term before, but, yes, that's exactly what it is."

She smiled at him. "But you have kids, so doesn't that apply to you?"

"Oh no, I'm divorced," he said, "and it wasn't a terribly pleasant one either."

"Is there such a thing?" she asked curiously.

"I have no idea," he said. "We married young, and I was gone a lot. She didn't like me being gone. So we separated and got back together a couple times. Then, when she got pregnant, we decided to give it a really good go." He shook his head. "We did for a while, ... and then we didn't," he said, with a shrug. "Probably should have walked the first time we separated but ..."

"Hindsight and all that," she murmured.

"Well, we were really good friends, and we should have stayed that way," he said. "I don't know what happened."

"I don't think you need to do a postmortem on it," she said. "It's enough to know that you're out of the situation now."

"Isn't that the truth?" He followed her directions, as she showed him the way to her place. When they got to the gate, she hopped out, opened it up, and he drove in. He waited on the other side, until she jumped back in again. "No electronics for that gate?"

"Yes, but I left it in my truck," she confessed. "And that's still in the shop."

"And when is it supposed to be ready?"

"It was supposed to be ready today, but it might not be till tomorrow now."

"Is this a case where the parts might accidentally go missing?"

"I hope not," she said, frowning, "but it has occurred to me that such a thing could happen."

"Well, let's hope not," he said, as he drove up to the ranch-style home and whistled. "Now this is my kind of a place."

"It was my father's," she said. "And his father's before him." When he looked at her in surprise, she nodded. "When I said I grew up around here, I meant it. My granddad built this house a good one hundred years ago," she said, with a smile. "He built it for his wife."

"Nice. It looks like it's had a few additions or renovations over the years."

"That it has," she said, with a laugh.

"Do you have any siblings?"

"No," she said, "it's just me."

At the house they quickly hopped out, and he locked up the truck, and they walked to the front door, where she started whistling.

"Dogs in or out?" he asked.

"They're mostly inside during the day," she said and quickly unlocked the front door. "But I have a dog run and a doggie door for them, so they're not cooped up all day long. With my job, I can be gone for hours on end." They stepped inside, to be greeted by three dogs, one a little more standoffish when it saw Bonaparte.

"It's okay, Max," she said, reaching down to gently scratch his ruffled neck. But he growled as he looked at Bonaparte. The big man immediately stilled, dropped to a knee, and held out his hand, giving the dogs as much time as they needed to accept him. The other two were racing all around him, jumping up, trying to make friends, and he was careful to pet them gently, but he kept his eye on the larger dog. "What is he?" he asked.

"A mutt," she said. "Max, it's okay. This is a friend."

Max sat down, looked over at Bonaparte, a whine in the back of his throat. Bonaparte immediately stretched his hand out a little farther.

"It's all right, buddy. I'm just here to help out." Almost immediately Max made a decision that Bonaparte was fine and came forward for a greeting. The two got to know each other very well, before Bonaparte slowly stood back up again, then looked around and nodded. "Nice place."

"A lot of years of history here," she said, with a smile. "A lot of good memories for me."

"In other words, you're not planning on leaving anytime soon."

"Never, I hope," she said.

"If they ask for your property?"

She walked into the kitchen and put on a pot of coffee.

"You want more coffee?" he asked curiously, leaning against the kitchen doorjamb.

She smiled and nodded. "Yes, I do." And then she shrugged and walked to the back and opened up a double set of French doors.

He and her dogs followed her through. Bonaparte whistled as he saw her backyard. "Wow," he said, "this is pretty fancy. So I noticed that you're ignoring my question about them wanting to purchase the land."

"Let me just say they've tried," she said.

"And I presume you declined."

"Yeah, because, in case you didn't notice," she said, "I'm one of the next properties in line here."

"So, the bottom line is, they need your land."

"Yeah."

"That's probably what this is all about then, right?"

"A lot of it, yes. I'm not sure if that's all of it though."

"It's quite enough," he said. "How much do you own?"

She sighed. "I have 160 acres." He just stared at her, dumbfounded. She shrugged. "There was a lot of family at one time, and it's pretty well all down to just me now."

"That's a lot of land," he said quietly.

She crossed her arms, leaned against one of the porch posts, and nodded. "It is."

"So, of course, you'll never sell."

"I'll never sell," she said, "and therefore—"

"Therefore, they need you to die in order to get this property." And he started to swear.

She watched him with interest. He was a huge man and generally very well controlled and contained, but right now this whole scenario was getting to him. "I see now that you understand why Levi sent you."

"He knows about this?"

"Yes, and they've hooked up security for me," she said, "but you and I both know, if Ronnie and Johnny want to take me out, they'll take me out."

"Goddammit," he said, staring at her. "It's got nothing to do with the town. It has everything to do with property, and you're in the prime place. It's got nothing to do with you being the sheriff even. It's all about you owning what they want."

"Yep, but you also can see that there's absolutely no way I can sell."

"Of course not," he said. "This is your heritage."

"It is."

"No other family?" he asked, as he watched the dogs playing in the yard.

"We've been a family of one child every time it got handed down," she said. "I was hoping to break the pattern. My mother actually had another sibling who died, and my grandfather had four kids, but only one made it to adulthood."

"With all this land around here, do you have any horses?"

"No, not now," she said, with a smile. "My grandfather used to train them here. A lot of the property is currently in farmland, which I have several local people operate for me," she murmured. "We've got orchards off to the left." She pointed with her arm. "If I wanted to, I could make it a pretty self-sufficient area."

"Which is probably what your grandfather thought about."

"He did, absolutely. We've got forty acres in hay," she said. "And I've got a good twelve acres in agriculture at this point, and I'm looking at putting more in. We've got twenty-plus acres in woods, and we've another twenty acres protecting a large stream and a small lake," she murmured. "I get it stocked with trout every once in a while, but I think I'm just feeding the wildlife around there more than actually providing for fishing."

"Fishing would be fun," he said. "Nobody told me that you were wealthy, wealthy."

"Not too many people know. They know about the land, but I don't think they necessarily equate that with money. I've got the house, but it's not like it's a multimillion-dollar home, like some places of this size have."

"No, your value is in the land."

"Exactly. And, to be honest, Ronnie's offer was generous," she said. "It's just that they don't like being turned down."

"And you have no intention of changing that."

"Nope, I don't, and they know that. There's only one way to get it away from me."

"But it's only you now," he said, shaking his head. "That makes me even more leery."

"Maybe," she said, "but I think that's also why they were checking out the new deputy and why they were so quick to run off my other deputies."

"And what's happening now? Surely you're getting new

ones."

"Yep, I'm trying to find somebody who will watch my back. I've told the town that more are coming because, of course, there is still crime happening in town, and the people all want to know they're safe too." Out of the blue she said, "The pool was something my father added," more to change the line of conversation than anything. "And then it was redone not too many years before he and my mom passed away," she murmured.

He looked at her sideways, picking up on a change in her. "When was that?"

Her lips pinched together. "Three years ago," she said and shrugged. "I expected them to have quite a few more years, but sometimes life isn't quite so kind."

"Anything in particular?"

She looked at him in surprise, then shrugged and said, "My mother was a Type 1 diabetic. She died from complications of that, and my father, he ended up with a bad bout of pneumonia and passed away not too long after her. He'd always had a compromised airway."

"I'm sorry," he said. "That must have been really tough."

"It was tough for me because I was the only one left behind, but the fact that they both passed so close together was better for them in the end because they didn't have to live without the other. They were really very close."

"Yeah, death is always harder for those left behind."

"Well, I hope so," she said, with a smile. "Otherwise, I'll have to start rethinking my view of hell."

He burst out laughing. "Now don't start doing that," he said. He looked at the huge yard. "This is a beautiful place to raise a family."

"It was a great place to grow up. I always planned to

have a big family too," she said. "But here I am, thirty-two and still single. One of my mother's greatest frustrations. If I could have found somebody before she died, it would have made them both very happy."

"Life doesn't happen on demand," he said. "I've got two kids, and, well, it's not quite the way I expected my life to end up either."

"Of course not, but we adapt, and we move on, and we hope that life changes in a good way," she said. "Since we already had that great dinner, I'll leave you to go for a swim, take a walk, or whatever you want to do. Please, just make yourself at home."

"I want to check out the property," he said.

"Levi was actually here a year ago or so. He talked me into some security," she said, "but he's been bugging me to do more."

"Hell, yes, you should be doing more!" he said. "Sorry, I didn't mean to bark at you. But seriously, with all the problems happening right now, you really should beef it up all you can."

"Yeah, I get that, but then there's the money issue. I'm land rich and cash poor."

"Oh, damn. Are you broke?"

"No," she said, "I'm not broke by any means, but it's not like I have a ton to spare just now."

"Right," he said, "and there is definitely a difference."

She watched in amazement as he moved about and studied the area, the dogs trailing behind him. He really had that look down pat. As if nothing escaped his gaze. She'd often asked Levi if any single guys were in his corner. It had been a bit of a running joke, but he always said he just hadn't found the perfect guy for her yet. She could imagine how Levi must have teased poor Bonaparte in advance of him getting here. It's not that she was desperate by any means because she wasn't, and she had enjoyed a really good brother-sister-type relationship with Levi that had continued to prosper over the years.

But she had to wonder if he hadn't been a little serious about Bonaparte. There was just something really appealing about a guy who was bigger than you. Particularly as tall as she was and with the history throughout her life of fending off the various jokes about being on stilts or towering over potential boyfriends. It didn't help that her mother was quite horrified when she continued to grow to the height she had, but thankfully she had eventually filled out a bit and got a few curves.

Her father on the other hand had always been damn proud of her height, size, and build. He had always wanted a son, and she'd done her best to fill his dreams for him. Now they were her dreams too, and one of them was never moving off this land. This was her home, and she couldn't imagine living anywhere else. She had told the overeager buyers as much, through the agents they had sent, not that she'd ever been approached by the actual would-be buyers. She told the agents quite clearly that she had no intention of selling ever. They had come back again and again and had increased the offer each time, but she just wasn't interested.

So, she was land rich and cash poor, like she'd said, but this was home. It had been home to her people for generations, and it wasn't changing anytime soon. But, because of all that had happened, she had had a will drawn up. And her Last Will and Testament did not allow for the property to be sold. It would be a charity in trust that would keep it as a private reserve. She also put in a bunch of other stipulations, just to make sure that, even if something did happen to her, it wouldn't benefit these guys who had caused such havoc in her county.

She hadn't told Bonaparte that. As he wandered the backyard, studying the pool, the layout, the trees, and the lines of sight, she could damn near see the way his thoughts were going, and she realized she didn't want to give up on that dream of having a family either. Not now, not ever. If nothing else, she felt she owed it to her lineage to keep it going one way or another. The fact that Bonaparte was here and was so damn attractive, made that much more of a prominent goal.

BONAPARTE LOVED THE land here. There were very few places in the world that he didn't like but this? This had a special pull. He wandered the area, taking great delight in the groves of trees that gave a lot of shade but kept the view open and gave the homesite the ability to look across acres and acres of land. The backyard was done beautifully, with stamped concrete around a huge pool and lots of space for dogs, for people partying, or for just having that whole family-barbecue thing. He could envision scenes filled with children and friends. He loved it and felt absolutely every-thing about it was first-rate. She was a very lucky woman.

But he also understood how close she was to losing it all. He would have to ask her about a will and what she had in place if she died because there was no way to take it with you, even though people have tried time and time again. Meanwhile, he would do anything he could to help her keep it. This was stunningly gorgeous and was her family history. No one on earth deserved to own this land more than her. It was her birthright, and nobody should force it away from her. She'd lost everything else and didn't deserve to lose this too.

He studied the area, looking for any security weaknesses, and of course there were plenty. When you had space like this, that meant anybody could come from any side. Even if she did have security around the house, it didn't stop anybody from coming cross-country and getting into the spaces you didn't want them to. He also needed to see if she had rifles or firepower of any kind beyond the standard-issue guns she carried on the job.

As he walked back, he studied the access from the gates around the side and definitely saw a few loopholes. Even though Levi had been here, more needed to be done. Of course it looked totally different now through the lens of an imminent threat. As he walked up to the long veranda, she sat there, a big pitcher beside her. He looked at it and smiled. "Lemonade?"

"Well, yes, with a bit of a twist," she said. "It's got gin in it. Would you like a glass?"

"Hell yes, that sounds great," he said, with a smile, as she poured him a cup and handed it to him. "Well, I walked around a bit. This is really a beautiful place."

"It is," she said, "and I really don't want to lose it."

"No, I don't think you should lose it at all." He studied the surroundings. "This is awkward and insensitive maybe, but, well, … have you made any arrangements?"

Angela immediately knew what he meant. She didn't evade the question and answered honestly. "Yes. It's not to be sold," she said. "It's to go to a charity in a trust for gardens, agriculture use, and that sort of thing. It's never to be used for development."

He smiled and nodded. "That's perfect and will just piss off Ronnie and Johnny even more."

"Maybe, but, if they've done something to me, thinking they'll get their hands on my property, you can sure as hell bet I'll do everything I can to make sure they don't. Even from the grave."

"Well, they won't get their hands on it," he said.

"I like your optimism," she said, "but I'm little more pragmatic than you are."

"I can see that," he said, "and I get it. I really do. That doesn't mean it's not doable though."

"Maybe," she said. "Or maybe not." With a weary smile, she said, "Come on. I'll show you where your room is."

He followed her up the stairs, loving the huge wide staircase and seeing the years of footprints going up and down. It was stunning. Not so much that it was a high-end house but that it was the heritage and the soul of the home. There was spirit to it, revealing the decades of love and dedication that had lived within. It was really hard to even imagine how anybody could abuse such a beautiful place, and the idea of someone leveling it was a horrible thought.

She opened the door to a room at the top of the stairs.

He walked in and smiled. "This is huge."

"This is the spare room," she said. "Mine is twice this size."

There was a dry note to her tone, and he looked at her and laughed. "Your grandpa or dad or somebody really liked to have some space."

"Mom and Dad both liked their space," she said. She nodded at a door on the far side of the room and said, "There's a small en suite for you over there too."

"Perfect," he said. "I'll go to my truck and grab my bag."

"Awesome," she said, then pointed down the hallway to the other end and said, "That's the master."

He could see double doors that were open. "I presume you have a big en suite in there."

"I do," she said, with a smile. "It's kind of ridiculous really." She hesitated and then said, "Listen. You do need to know that we've had a few random shootings into the house itself." He stopped and stared. She nodded. "And I've got nobody to report it to."

"Except another sheriff, the district attorney, or somebody."

"True, but I haven't been able to find a damn bullet."

"That would be frustrating," he said. "Any chance they came back later and got it?"

"If they knew where they shot it, maybe," she said. "The siding isn't exactly conducive to finding a small hole, so I haven't found it, which doesn't give me any evidence to use against whoever it is when I finally catch them."

"No," he said, "but I'll keep an open mind on that."

She nodded. "Just a friendly warning."

"Hey, this place is just full of joy," he said, with a laugh.

"That it is," she said.

They walked back downstairs, and he headed out the front door, where he opened up his truck, grabbed his bag, and hauled it inside. The dogs followed him out and back in again.

She smiled and said, "Looks like they've made another friend."

"Most dogs feel that way," he said, "as long as you're no threat to them and those they love."

"You're no threat to me," she said easily.

"Did you even check with Levi to make sure I really

work there?"

"As soon as you walked in the Sheriff's Department," she said.

He burst out laughing. "I'm sure he appreciated that."

"You both would have had my hide if I hadn't." She grinned. "I might be under the gun on a few things, but I'm not stupid."

"Never that," he said. "No need to worry. We'll get behind this."

"Nothing to get behind," she said. "But we'll have to get ahead, stop some of their attacks, and find a way to put them behind bars. Or at least pick them up so that they're not threatening people."

"But nobody has even caught on to the fact that they've been threatened, have they?"

"Not directly, no," she said. "My girlfriend today was the first one."

"And that's not even so much of a threat, since it would be easy to put that off to her being paranoid or just high-strung."

"Exactly," she said, "and that doesn't help anybody."

He wondered about her words a long time later, as he lay in his bed, listening to the sounds of nature cackling and howling around him. He loved it. He loved everything about it. But, then again, he was all about open spaces and freedom, and that's what this place offered. It was stunning, and he could see why someone would want to take it from her. But the fact that those same people might want to level, raze the whole thing, and put up something like multilevel condos just made him sick to his stomach. He pulled out his phone and updated Levi, with the little bit Bonaparte knew so far.

Rather than text back, Levi phoned him. "She's a good person," he said. "Do all you can for her."

"I hear you," he said. "She's pretty special. I'll give you that. But the scenario is damn strange."

"I know," he said. "That's one of the reasons she needs help. There's a lot of pressure from a lot of areas because these guys have significant influence. They have money, and they're getting people who wouldn't normally cause her trouble to cause her trouble."

"Nobody's on her side from the looks of it either."

"No, it's more a case of she survives, or she doesn't. Nobody'll really care either way."

"And that's unbelievable, considering she's been here her whole life. Where are her neighbors?"

"Most of them moved on," Levi said. "That area was hit pretty rough economically a few years ago, and they lost a lot of the younger people."

"Surely some of the old-timers will be there for her."

"I wouldn't count on it," Levi said.

"It's a damn sad state of affairs if that's the truth," he said. "Somebody out here should be helping her at all times."

"There is somebody," he said, "there's you." Then he hung up.

Bonaparte fell asleep not long afterward. With a smile on his face. But the smile wasn't there when he woke to an odd sound. True, he was in an area he wasn't familiar with, and the completely natural noises all around him were some that he didn't recognize. But *that noise*, he did. It was the sharp *ping* of a bullet. He slipped out of bed and pulled on his jeans, checking out the window from its side and saw nothing, before he slipped down the stairs, heading for the front door. He bypassed the door and went to one of the big windows on the side and checked outside from a corner. Absolutely nothing was in the driveway, not that he could see as he walked around the house checking out the other windows. He reached the back door to find Angela, leaning against the doorjamb, rifle in hand.

"Was that you?" he asked quietly.

"No," she said. "It was him, up there." She pointed.

Even as he watched, he caught a wink of shiny metal. "Jesus," he said, "that's a dead giveaway."

"Yeah, and that shot went into the house."

"And yet you're standing here in a clear line of sight?"

"As is the rifle," she said.

"You don't think he'll get you there?" he asked, cautiously looking at her in surprise.

"I don't think so, but I could be wrong."

He wondered just where this was going.

She looked at him, smiled, and said, "Enough barriers are between here and there," she said, "that I don't think he can get to me." But she stepped back and said, "And I haven't been out here for very long."

"Any time is too long," he said, "if he has any idea what he's doing."

"Well, that should have proven to you that he's not capable because that shot was a good ten minutes ago."

"It did wake me," he admitted.

"I'm not surprised," she said. "A sound like that is something you recognize for the rest of your life."

"And yet there's no sign of who it is?"

"No, not at all. And I know, by the time I get out there, he'll be long gone."

"How far can he go?"

"Well, miles in any direction, in theory. And to their

own property, if it's the brothers," she said. "It isn't all that far. Maybe three miles cross country."

"And it's a clear night with a full moon," he added.

"Exactly."

"So what is the purpose? Just to make you nervous or something?"

"Well, I've wondered that myself," she said. "I can't see how they would think that would be very effective. I've spent a lifetime here, and I work in law enforcement, so I hardly think a stray bullet will make a difference."

"And what about when they start killing your dogs?" he asked.

She nodded. "Oh, don't worry. I've thought of that too. And, of course, it'll make me mad as hell. If I could prove who it is, I'd have stopped them by now. But you know what it's like to get proof on something like that. With the dogs, I'll come home one day, and it will be done."

He frowned at that, as he looked down at the happy dogs milling at his feet. "You know it's a shitty thing that people do just to hurt you."

"It's the shady things that people do as a warning," she said. "Abusing animals to hurt their human owners. Because people suck."

"That they do," he murmured, then sighed. "If you tell me where to go, I could certainly go out and take a look."

"I was just getting my boots on," she said, pointing down. "I'm watching to see which direction he goes."

As Bonaparte stared at her, she smiled and said, "Really, I'm not giving up by any means. But I do have a good idea of who this is and what he's doing. If that shiny reflection moves in that direction," she said, "it's the guy Ronnie from the restaurant." Even as they watched, they saw another wink of steel moving in the right direction. She nodded. "Bull's-eye." She immediately stepped into her boots, and then, with her rifle in hand and the dogs beside her, she stepped off the porch and headed in that direction.

"Whoa, whoa, whoa," he said. "Where are you going?"

"To have a talk with my neighbor," she said and didn't slow down at all.

It was all he could do to grab his own gear, and, without even a shirt on, he raced behind her. "The least you could do is wait for me."

"You don't have to come," she said. "This is my fight, not yours."

He snorted at that. "You can stop that line of thinking right now," he said. "That's bull."

"If you want to come along, your company is welcome. Just so you know what you're getting into."

"Oh, I know what I'm getting into," he said. "The shit falls not very far from the stick, and, in this case, we saw the stick."

She laughed at that. "You could be right," she said, "but I've never been able to catch him."

"And you don't really seem to think you will now either, do you?"

"Nope," she said. "This is just a game to them, and I'm not even sure it's them, versus a hired hand."

"Which would be even worse, since that would be murder for hire."

"You know what? I'm not sure if that's even the case yet," she said, frowning. "I think they could have done a better job if it were murder for hire. They could have taken me out anytime."

"Yet they haven't. So why is that?"

"I think it's the last resort honestly," she said. "I think they want the property, but they're hoping to get it without having to kill me."

"Well, that would certainly reduce their exposure, wouldn't it?"

"It would," she said cheerfully, "but it won't work. So how long until they give up on that idea?"

Chapter 5

ANGELA HAD SEEN this time and time again, only she didn't walk out in the middle of the night afterward. But tonight? She was just fed up and pissed off enough that she wanted to see if her shooter would really go to the property she thought he was. Angela stomped through the brush, not even making any attempt to stay calm or quiet.

"You want to make this a little more stealthy in our approach?" he asked.

"Nope," she said, "I don't."

He just shrugged and let her go.

She appreciated that; it was a sign of a mutual respect growing between them. When they finally got to the neighbor's place, she studied the layout, looking to see any changes made to the place. Lights were definitely on in the kitchen, projecting into the backyard. She walked a wide perimeter around the house, which was close to her property's boundary. Another reason Ronnie probably wanted her land. There were all kinds of reasons, but she didn't have to make excuses. They wanted it, but they couldn't have it, so they would be immature about it.

Just then, on the far side, she watched somebody open a gate and step through.

Instantly Bonaparte stiffened beside her. "There's our shooter."

"Yeah, it sure is," she said, "but I need that rifle to prove it."

"That's easy enough," he said and disappeared from sight. She swore silently, as he melted around the corner and, like a shadow, blended from tree to tree to tree.

As the shooter stopped and stretched, he rotated his shoulders and neck, then placed the rifle on the ground beside him and just stood there for a long moment. A dog came out of the house and raced toward him. He gave it a big long cuddle, as if he had been waiting for the dog to come. When he started to get up, he reached for the gun, stopped, looked around, and looked again. The rifle was gone. Then he started to swear. The dog at his side started to bark and bark.

Somebody from inside the house stepped out. "Honey, is that you?"

"Go back to bed. I told you not to wait up for me," the man yelled.

"When you go out of the house in the middle of the night, what do you expect me to do?" The woman's voice had a plaintive tone.

Angela studied the woman but didn't recognize her, although that wasn't surprising, since women came and went with a scary regularity. The man just swore at her and said, "Get the fuck in the house. Somebody's out here."

"No, there isn't," she said. "It was just you. Come on in. You can have a drink and relax."

"No!" he said. "Just do as I say and go inside."

"Don't be so grouchy. Come on. I know you're just going out there and taking potshots at coyotes," she said, "and I presume the hunting didn't go all that well, or you'd be in a better mood."

"Do I have a gun with me?" he snapped, as he walked closer.

"Well, you did when you left," she said, with a very clear *don't speak to me in that tone of voice* attitude behind her words.

He glared. "Just pack up and get the hell out of my house," he said.

"Well, it's not my fault the hunting didn't go well," she snapped. "You don't have to blame me."

"Hell," he said, "you better go pack up and get out of here, before I decide that you become the next hunt."

She gasped at that. "Don't you dare talk to me that way. Are you calling me an animal?"

He just looked at her, and Angela could see from the light of the kitchen door that he was still struggling with what his latest bimbo was thinking. Angela wanted to laugh out loud, yet it was hardly a laughing matter if he ended up turning the gun on the woman. Except for the fact that there was no gun because it had disappeared. Even now, as he was yelling at her to get into the house, he was looking around for the rifle, but there was no sign of it.

Meanwhile, the dog was tripping him up, thinking this was a new game. He was barking and jumping into the whole mess. Angela stood here, her dogs on alert but staying silent on her orders, watching in amazement, as this calm and organized-looking killer just lost it. Before she had a chance to consider that further, Bonaparte was at her side.

"Well, I've got the rifle," he said. "Did you want to stay and watch the show?"

"Nope," she said. "I've seen enough. It was great, but now I want to go home."

So together they slid into the darkness, this time retracing their steps with a silence that she appreciated. When they got back to her house, she looked at the rifle and realized that he wore gloves. "Where'd you get those?" she asked.

"Oh, I keep an emergency pair or two in my pocket all the time," he said. "You never know when you'll come across some evidence, or you don't want to leave any," he said, with a smirk. "Now we'll find out where the bullets are."

"Yeah, I haven't figured that part out yet," she said.

"We'll find them tomorrow," he promised.

She looked at him in surprise. "You're awfully confident. How do you propose to do that?"

He grinned broadly. "Metal detector."

She was both astonished and gratified because that could work. "If you could do that, it would give me the first bit of proof. As long as we can match the bullet to this barrel, of course."

"I presume you can get that done at work?"

"Yeah," she said. "I sure can."

"Good enough," he said. "Tomorrow it is. Now, go get some rest," he said. "We've got a big day tomorrow."

"We do?"

"Absolutely," he said. "There's a pool to dive into, and I'd love to explore the area."

She smiled. "That would be good," she said. "Generally it's just me out there."

"I can see how that's probably been lonely as hell for you. But I'm here now, so we can liven things up a little bit," he said. "You've got a nice barbecue pit out there. Can I cook on it?"

"Sure," she said. "What do you want to make?"

"Got any ribs?" he asked, as he waggled his eyebrows at her.

"Oh, stop," she said, laughing.

"I love, love, love barbecue. So, if we get the ribs," he said, "I'll take over cooking dinner tomorrow night."

"You're on," she said. "It's the weekend anyway, but I should warn you. Since I have no deputies, you can count on the fact that I'll get called out."

"Well, where you get called, I'm going as well," he said. "We are not to be apart. Do you hear me?"

She nodded. "Is that your dictate, or is it Levi's?"

"Both of us."

"He does realize that I can take care of myself, right?"

"Of course he does," he said, "and so do I. But remember. We all need help occasionally. Sometimes shit goes the wrong way, and it doesn't matter who we are or what capabilities we have. Bullets really aren't discerning. They'll take us all out, one way or another."

"Good enough, as long as you don't believe I can't handle this."

"I believe it," he said. "I do. You have nothing to prove, and we all need help sometimes. In this case Levi knows just how bad things are, and he sent me to give you a hand."

She nodded, with a smile. "And it's appreciated," she said. "Honestly it is."

"No doubt," he said. "Now go to bed. Tomorrow's a whole new day." She smiled, and, with the dogs traipsing upstairs beside her, she headed to bed. Quickly she switched out of the clothes she'd thrown on and lay down on the bed. The little dogs came up beside her, and Max lay down at her feet.

"It's okay, Max," she murmured. He rarely slept anymore. The potshots in the dark made him a little more edgy, a little more disgruntled throughout the day, but he was always listening for those intruders that they both knew were out there, just waiting for a chance to pounce.

"We made it through another night, buddy, and, with Bonaparte here, we should at least get some sleep." *Maybe for the first time in a very long time,* she thought to herself. At least since all this shit came down. How the hell had her life gotten so warped? She'd been the sheriff for eight years, one of the youngest ever hired in the area. In all that time, she'd been doing a damn good job, as far as she was concerned; and, so far, the town had agreed. But somewhere along the line it had turned into a mess, and she knew exactly who to blame. She wanted her town cleaned up, and she wanted back again the confidence and the respect she'd worked so hard to earn from the townsfolk. But getting there looked like it would be a little more difficult than she had anticipated.

Maybe with Bonaparte giving her a hand, she could pull this off. She damn well hoped so. But, like he'd said, everybody needs a little help sometimes. Because, along with being the sheriff and having her property here, this is where she wanted to stay, ... for the rest of her life. She wasn't sure if she would still have a way to make a living wage after the next election, but she'd figure out something. Hopefully she wouldn't have to seek alternate employment because it would be awfully hard to tackle anything different when her heart and soul were committed to this work. Right along with this property that was her heritage and maybe going the self-sustaining route. With that thought uppermost in her mind, she fell asleep.

BONAPARTE WOKE UP the next morning, rested and raring

to go. He jumped out of bed, pulled on a change of clothes, and went downstairs. Even as he got there, he found her up and sitting outside, with a cup of coffee. He stared at her in disgruntlement. "You know what? I used to be the first person up," he said. "I don't know too many people who are up before me."

"Well then, you've never been here before, have you?" she said, getting up, heading inside with a smile.

"I guess not. Why are you up so early?"

"I'm always up early," she murmured, refilling her coffee mug. "It goes along with the dogs. And the life."

"Well, the life maybe," he said. "I can see that. Anything happen while I slept?"

"Nope. Everything is calm," she said, reaching for another cup, "deceptively so."

"The calm before the storm?" he asked.

"Yeah. What will you do today?" she asked, as she poured him a coffee, then headed back outside.

Bonaparte followed her to the patio table and sat beside her. "I've ordered a metal detector. It's supposed to come in today," he said. "I'll go to town pick it up."

"I'll come with you," she said.

"You don't think I can handle it?"

"No, I just want to see people's reactions," she said, leaning back in her chair.

"You don't want to stay here alone and enjoy some downtime?"

"Not sure that's even possible," she said. "When they start taking potshots in the middle of the night," she noted, "you know they'll be up for most anything."

"Yeah," he said. "They could also burn down your house."

"I've thought of that," she said. "I raised my homeowner's coverage just in case."

"Right. Because it's still just a house, isn't it?"

"I could rebuild if I had to," she said. "I wouldn't want to, but I could."

"You know what? I think it's a better idea if you do come with me," he said. "Maybe we'll take the dogs along too."

"Why is that?"

"Because then I can keep an eye on all of you," he said, with a bright smile.

"No, they are fine here. This is their home." She laughed. "I checked out the freezer, and we don't have enough ribs."

He groaned in mock despair. "In that case, we'll definitely go to town."

"What do you want first? The ribs or your package?"

"The longer we have the ribs marinating, the better," he said. "So we can go now, or we can wait a little bit and see if that parcel is in."

"It'll take a miracle to get a parcel in that fast," she said. "But I'd rather do only one trip."

"Miracles happen," he said. "This is Levi. Remember?"

"And that's true. If anybody can get this stuff done fast, it would be Levi and Ice."

"Levi and Ice are a hell of a pair, aren't they? And Ice makes things happen. Stuff that you wouldn't believe even possible."

Angela nodded. "Ice and I have become good friends," she said, "but we're just far enough away that we don't get to visit."

"Not sure any visiting happens anytime," he said, "unless

you live in the compound."

"Must be a few dozen people living there now, at least, isn't there?"

"Oh, yes, every bit of that," he said and laughed. "But it's a fun environment."

"For a lot of people," she said, "unless you're the kind who wants space." She motioned to the area around her.

"Not many people have this option," he said, as he surveyed all that surrounded them. He checked his watch. "What time does anything open in town?"

"Not for hours," she said. "We're early."

"Damn," he said. "I was hoping to go grab the stuff we needed and get home."

"We will, but we might as well have breakfast first."

"Oh." He looked at her with interest. "What do you have in mind?"

She snorted. "If you're like the rest of Levi's crew, anything that's food will do nicely."

"That's true, but we all consider ourselves gourmets, with Alfred and Bailey there."

She snorted at that again. "You guys are just plain spoiled."

He grinned. "I can cook too."

"Well, ribs at least," she said, "but I've got sausage and bacon, hash browns and eggs. So you tell me what you want."

"Yes."

She stared at him for a minute, then burst out laughing, and, hopping to her feet, she said, "Got it. But do you always eat like this?"

"Every chance I get," he said, with a bright smile.

She shook her head and led the way back inside, where

she poured two more cups of coffee, brought out a frying pan, and started working on the sausage.

"We don't have to have both bacon and sausage, if you don't want to."

"I've just got a few sausages left, so I can fry them up before they go bad," she said. "So we'll have bacon too because I don't have enough sausages."

"Well, as long as there's plenty of something," he said, "I'll be perfectly happy to stay here and eat."

"So long as there's grub," she murmured.

He nodded. "That and good company."

She laughed again and shook her head. "I forget just how lonely life is out here now," she murmured.

"You should never be lonely," he said.

"Well, you are, when you face situations like this sometimes."

He stopped, thought about it, and then nodded. "That, unfortunately, is quite right. Nobody should have to face something like this alone."

"Well, I'm not alone now, am I?"

"Nope, you're not," he said, with a definite nod. "As long as you remember that, we'll be good."

Chapter 6

B Y THE TIME Bonaparte and Angela headed into town, the butcher shop was due to open in another ten minutes, and the post office would be a little bit after that. They still had to deal with pretty-lazy town hours, but they did the best they could, and she appreciated that. They went to the butcher first, and she bought two racks of ribs, but, as she went to pay for it, Bonaparte stepped in and paid instead. She looked at him with a sideways glance. He shrugged, and then he ordered more bacon, and, as he wandered around, he picked up two big steaks.

"When do you want the steaks?" she asked.

"Tomorrow night," he said. He tapped the glass case. "You know what? We could use some stuff for sandwiches too."

"Hey, if you're always hungry, you're the one who needs to pick up enough stuff to fill that stomach of yours." She could tell that the butcher was more than a little interested in everything they were doing. She had never really been known to have much of a boyfriend. She had dated and had a few relationships, but nothing that would ever cause a commotion like this guy would. Not only was he her deputy but he was huge.

She smiled over at Ross and said, "Looks like I'll be getting a little bit more than normal."

He just nodded and rang it up, but his gaze flicked from Bonaparte to her and then back again. But he was too polite to say anything. Bonaparte quickly paid for the rest and then moved the purchases outside. "I figured he might have said something," Bonaparte murmured.

"He was probably too afraid of what you might say back."

Bonaparte nodded. "I do tend to have that effect on people."

"In that case, I should make you come shopping with me all the time," she said. "I think we got faster service too."

"I'm not sure about faster," he said. "The store was empty."

"Yeah, but normally he dawdles and likes to talk and take his time."

"Well, socializing with you is probably off the table now," he said.

"That could be," she murmured. Next they drove to the gas station, where Bonaparte filled up the truck. "We'll head to the post office next."

"I don't think I'll have anything there," she said.

"Mine came in by courier," he said, checking his phone. "Got confirmation of arrival."

"So we'll go there afterward," she said, with a nod. By the time they had collected everything they needed in town, they had caused quite a stir, with various people stepping out on the sidewalk to watch them. She smiled and called out to a few of the locals, who more or less inclined their heads at her but studied Bonaparte warily.

"So are they scared of you?" she asked. "Is that a normal reaction?"

"Well, I'm not exactly putting out friendly vibes," he

said. "I don't want them to chalk up my being here as your boyfriend and thus not as great a threat to them."

"I think they've been threatened enough," she said, choosing to bypass his boyfriend comment.

He smiled. "Maybe, and maybe that's not a bad idea anyway."

She just shrugged. As they hopped into the truck for the last time, she said, "Don't look now, but we have company."

He pulled out onto the road and said, "Are they likely to follow?"

She checked her side mirror and said, "Looks like they are." And, sure enough, a big Hummer pulled in behind them, as they headed toward home.

"Interesting," he said. "Not local kids here. The Hummer speaks to money. So somebody hired from out-of-town?"

"Makes sense."

"Will they just follow us in?"

"Unless they've got firepower," she said quietly.

He looked at her sharply and immediately punched his foot down hard on the gas pedal. The Hummer came flying up behind them as well. Bonaparte turned sharply around in the middle of the street, too fast for the Hummer to hit the brakes. By the time the Hummer even realized Bonaparte had bypassed him, Bonaparte was back on the road, behind the Hummer at the same speed.

"That was a pretty nifty maneuver," she said in surprise.

"Yeah, it is," he said, "and sometimes, when you get ass-holes on your tail, you need to know how to do a few of these."

"In that case," she said, "maybe you could show me one or two."

"Absolutely," he said. They drove down the road, but now the Hummer had slowed, figuring out what to do.

"Do you think he'll try the same thing?" Angela asked.

"He's not fast enough," Bonaparte said calmly. Sure enough, the Hummer tried to pull off to the side, and Bonaparte just pulled off at the same time. When the Hummer pulled back onto the road and tried to go to the opposite side, Bonaparte followed him. She wanted to laugh because it's exactly what the Hummer was trying to do to them. But, in this case, the rattler got rattled. "He's likely to just drive home to his house."

"And that's fine," he said calmly. "We've got one weapon, and I've got a job to do at home to find those bullets. But, in the meantime, I'm not interested in being somebody's prey."

"We'll just piss him off," she said.

"If we piss him off, he'll do something fast and stupid."

"You mean, more stupid," she said. "They've always been just at the edge of the law. Nobody ever really crosses the line, so I can't do much."

"Yeah, you get guys like that sometimes, who know exactly what they're doing."

"And it's irritating," she said, "because I know that the rest of the town is looking at me to do something, to stay out of it and leave them alone, or to throw in the towel and walk away."

"Not your style," he said calmly.

"No, it sure isn't," she said, loving that he actually got it.

"Besides," he murmured, "I'm not into letting assholes take over a place like this and do stuff like that. It's not cool."

"It doesn't matter if it's cool or not," she said. "Money

can buy quite a lot of leeway."

"It does, and too often guys like this get away with that crap, but we won't let them."

Her emotions were bolstered immediately at his positive tone. "I wonder how long you're planning on staying then?" she asked, almost as an afterthought.

He looked at her in surprise. "How long do you think this will take?" he asked.

"I don't know," she said, studying him. "Depends what game plan you have."

"You see? That's the problem. We don't have one yet," he said. "We're still getting our defenses going and figuring out just what we do have for a plan."

"You mean, options," she said, with a shrug.

"We need more history on these guys, so I'm waiting for Levi to get back to us on that."

"I've asked him for a bunch of information too," she said. "And I've talked to a couple of my bosses. Just to see what options I have."

"Do you have bosses?"

She shrugged. "Really the people are my boss because I'm voted in, and I can get voted out, but it's more than that. There are laws that these assholes aren't allowed to cross."

"But they've already crossed them, haven't they?"

She nodded. "They have, yes, but I have nothing to pick them up for, as I have no proof."

"And, if you did pick them up, you couldn't keep them, and all it will do is cause trouble and make it look like you're weak and inefficient."

"Which is what they're already doing," she admitted.

"Right, because you don't have a good legal leg to take a stand against them."

"Well, I should be able to, but again I don't have any real reason, outside of making it look like I'm hassling them."

"Got it," he said.

"Have you got a siren on this thing?"

"I sure do. Why?"

"Because he's missing a taillight. That should be plenty of grounds for pulling him over."

At that, he reached over, hit the siren, and sped up, putting pressure on the Hummer to either pull off to the side of the road or try to escape. And, sure enough, he stepped on the gas and took off.

"Wow," she said, "I didn't think he would run."

"And the fact that he is makes me very curious as to why," he said, stepping on the gas. "Well, this old girl's still got some juice in her," he remarked, as they were able to quickly catch up to the Hummer.

"That she does," she said. He kept on driving behind the Hummer, staying up tight. They were almost up to the two properties recently bought by the asshole brothers, when she said, "I wonder if he'll try to go on past, hoping that we'll go home."

"It doesn't matter what he's hoping for," Bonaparte said, holding steady.

"Well," she said, "we'll find out soon enough." And, just as she said that, the Hummer blew a tire, just ahead of them. It fishtailed several times, back and forth on the road, its brakes flashing off and on, off and on. Then finally it spun around out of control and came to a stop, half in and half out of the ditch on the side of the road. Bonaparte pulled up beside the wrecked Hummer, and Angela raced ahead, her handgun available and ready to pull, then popped open the driver's side door.

"What the hell," the driver said blearily, blood streaming off his forehead. "I'll have your badge for that, Sheriff."

"You blew a tire all on your own. Driver's license and insurance," she said in derision. "You were trying to elude the sheriff and her deputy."

"You are just hassling me," he said, "I didn't do anything to you."

"You're driving without functional taillights," she snapped.

"What?" He looked at her and over at Bonaparte, who shrugged.

"Your lights are out on the one side."

The driver tried to exit the vehicle.

"Hand over your DL and proof of insurance. Then you can exit your vehicle."

He grumbled, but he complied.

Angela wrote down the info on her ticket pad, showing Bonaparte the driver's name.

He snorted. "*John Smith*, huh? You can bet we'll dig deep to find out more about you." And Bonaparte promptly sent a copy of his DL and insurance papers to Levi.

The guy continued to moan, got out of the vehicle slowly, and stood up precariously. She reached over to grab him and asked, "Do you need an ambulance?"

He shrugged her off and said, "If I do, it's because of you."

"Not hardly," Bonaparte said. "We were pulling you over to ask you about the taillight not working."

He glared at him. "It was working this morning."

"Well, it isn't working now," Bonaparte said. "And then there's that tailgating earlier."

"I wasn't doing nothing. You were driving too slow, and I was trying to get home."

She looked at him with half a smile. "Really? Do you think that'll work in a court of law?"

He sneered at her. "You don't have anything on me, and I'll have your badge for putting me in the ditch."

"Not happening. In the meantime, you should take some driving lessons." She wrote him up a ticket for his taillight and said, "Get that fixed within forty-eight hours." He just glared at her, as she slapped it in his hand, and then she walked back over to the truck.

Bonaparte hopped in, and they turned around and drove to her property. "Did you know that guy? Ever seen him before?"

She shook her head. "Nope."

"He seems to own the Hummer, not renting it. So will he get it fixed?"

"It's a simple-enough thing, and he certainly should, but will he? I don't know," she said. "A citation for something like that is hardly a big step in any direction."

"No, but it still shows that he can get pinned by something as negligible as that," he said.

She shrugged. "But it doesn't make a damn bit of difference in the end. He'll be back doing some other shit before long anyway," she said, sounding frustrated.

"Hold steady," Bonaparte replied. "We'll find a way."

She looked over at him and said, "Sorry. I'm just out of patience and have no clue how we're supposed to make any of this happen."

"That's why I'm here."

"Maybe," she said, "but you haven't come up with any ideas yet either."

He winced. "Hey, since I've been here, we pushed Ronnie's buttons and flushed out a shooter. I'll now go hunt for the bullet," he said, as he drove up the long driveway to her home. "We've found some of the local teens who do Ronnie's and Johnny's bidding, plus the Hummer guy who's already pissed off that I'm here, enough that he's chasing us down the road. As a matter of fact, I happen to think we've chased quite a few bad guys out of the shadows."

"Maybe," she said, "but all of it is the same old shit."

"Well, I'm here now," he said, "so I won't deal with the same old shit. We'll find some bright shiny new shit."

At that, she burst out laughing and said, "This is a ridiculous conversation."

He looked over, grinned, and said, "I know, but you're smiling again."

She shook her head, feeling the same gloominess take over again. "I've got no business smiling," she said. "This is just a crap deal all around."

"But it's what we do," he said, "so we'll fix it."

She smiled, loving his positive attitude. And knowing that he was one of Levi's guys, she was willing to give him a little bit of rope. She didn't want it to be enough to hang him because she really, really wanted him to have some great ideas of what they could actually do here. Otherwise, she was afraid that, one night, she just wouldn't wake up.

As soon as they were home, greeted by all the dogs, and everything was unloaded, and he'd fussed with the ribs and the steaks, he grabbed the package that had been sent overnight from Levi. Bonaparte unpacked a metal detector, a small handheld unit without the long bar, but something useful for vertical applications. He systematically went over the relevant side of the house, thankful for the access Levi had to a unit that had a broad range and could even discern between different metals.

Because her home had old wood siding, clad with shingles, it was easy for a bullet to get missed by a visual check. He was into it about an hour, when he heard a distinctly different *ding* than it produced when he went over the nailing line. He stopped, refocused, studied the spot, marked it, and then went into the kitchen and asked if she had any tools. She quickly walked over to a large toolbox she kept in the pantry.

He dug around to find a screwdriver and a pair of pliers, then headed back out. She followed. Outside, he pointed where the machine had signaled. Gently they removed the shingle, and underneath they found the bullet. Carefully he pulled it out, looked at her, grinned, and said, "Now we need to check this against the rifle."

She nodded. "I'll take that in this afternoon and get it sent out."

"You're not going alone," he said. She looked at him in surprise. He shook his head. "You can't. Your vehicle is still in the shop," he said. "Besides it's not safe. There's just too much going on right now."

She shrugged. "In that case, I guess we're going back to town."

"Yep," he said cheerfully, "and that's okay too. The ribs are all settled in. I've got the steaks marinating for tomorrow night. I'm not sure where you're at for vegetables, but, if there happens to be any corn on the cob, that would be good," and he waggled his eyebrows.

She shook her head, smirking. "I didn't realize you were such a foodie."

"Of course I'm a foodie," he said. "I love food."

She rolled her eyes. "Well, we all love food," she said, with a chuckle.

"Yeah, but I really, really love food." He smiled and said, "So, is there any corn locally?"

"There might be," she said. "If not, we can head over to one of the farms where I often buy veggies."

"Good," he said, "we could just shop there instead of town."

"We'll see," she said. "Let's head to the station first and get this taken care of." They hopped into the truck and headed there. When they arrived, she unlocked the door and quickly took care of what she needed to do, then got out the materials to ship the evidence. She stopped and frowned. "Unless you want to go to Denver?" she said. "We can do the trip in and out, and I can drop this off at the main station there, where the ballistics staff can handle it."

He immediately nodded. "That would be best," he said. "Otherwise we'll be waiting even longer, right?"

She nodded and made a quick call, checking on her truck to find out it wouldn't be ready for another twenty-four hours. Frowning, she decided to leave that issue alone for now. "Yes, and dealing with all the shipping hassles," she said, "sometimes, if it's important, I do drive them in."

"Let's go," he said.

She nodded, quickly locked up, and, with both the weapon packed up in a case and the bullet in an evidence bag, they drove into Denver. On the way there, she asked him several questions about his family, his kids, and what he wanted to do with his life.

At that, he just laughed and said he was doing it. "I see my kids in the summer, and I work for Levi when I'm not with my kids."

"Does he just give you time off?"

"That's my agreement," he said, "my time with my kids is time off from Levi."

"As long as you can afford it," she said, looking at him sideways.

He shrugged. "I'll make it work," he said. "The kids are important."

She liked that about him. By the time they hit the station in Denver, and she had delivered both the weapon and the bullet and then documented the details in a report, they hopped back in.

"Do you want to grab some lunch while we're here?" he asked.

"We can," she said. "A nice burger place is up ahead."

"We can do that," he said. "I also wanted to pull some records from City Hall."

"It's Saturday," she said, with a shake of her head. "You won't get very far." He frowned at her, and she frowned right back. "It doesn't matter what you want to do. It's still a government site, and nobody will be interested in opening up for you on the weekend."

He groaned. "Fine, I'll have Levi get it for me."

"What are you looking for?"

"Recent transfers of property in your county, past and current owners, land use restrictions, mortgage holders, mechanics liens, that kind of thing."

"Get Levi to do as much as you can while he's at it," she said, "since they have connections that we don't."

"Isn't that interesting?"

"It really is."

"You know what?" he said. "While we're here, we might want to look at a few other things in town."

"Like?"

"Well, I'm not sure how you are for firepower."

"Meaning weapons?" she asked. "I've got a .22 and my police issue."

"Right," he said. "I also arranged with Levi to pick up a couple weapons somewhere else."

"What do you mean by *somewhere else?*"

He looked at her sideways. "At a friend's place."

She rolled her eyes at that. "Right, a *friend.*"

He laughed and said, "How about we do a stop-off, and I pick them up?"

"Sure. I thought you had a handgun with you."

"Well, I brought one here, yes," he said. "But we could always use a little more."

She just shrugged, as if it didn't matter.

He drove to a small shop and walked in to find one of Levi's friends, who looked up at him, smiled, and said, "You must be Bonaparte."

She looked over at him and asked, "Does everybody know you?"

"Hell no," he said, "but, in this case, it's a good thing." He introduced the two of them and said, "Richard, this is Sheriff Angela Zimmerman." They shook hands, and he continued, "Levi said that you had something here for me."

Richard nodded and picked up a weapons case, sitting off to the side, and said, "This one's for you." Bonaparte opened it up, looked at it, and whistled. "Oh, this will do perfectly. How much do I owe you?"

"Levi's already taken care of it."

"Nice to have friends like Levi," she said, with a smile.

"Don't forget. This is still a job for him. He supplies everything."

"I get that," she said. "It's just irritating in a way."

"Don't let it irritate you," he said. "That's what friends are for. Sometimes we need everything our friends can offer."

"Well, right now I certainly do," she murmured. She watched as Richard added ammo to the case and packed up the weapon. She faced Bonaparte and said, "But we don't have a license for it."

Bonaparte looked to Richard, who immediately pulled out the paperwork and a side holster for the weapon and handed it to him.

She looked at it in surprise, then at him and asked, "How did you get that?"

"Legally," Bonaparte said. "We travel all the time with weapons. If I had driven here, I would have brought more than I could have flying."

She nodded slowly and said, "I don't need to think about it, do I?"

"I'm here with all the paperwork in hand." He signed for their receipt, and then they left again.

She looked at him sideways. "Does Levi really have ways to do all this?"

He looked at her in surprise and then nodded. "In every state in the country and in most of the countries in the world. Obviously not all because we haven't been to every one at this point in time." He tilted his head in consideration. "You know what? That would be an interesting question to ask him, whether we've completed jobs in every country or not."

"I guess," she murmured. "I didn't realize just how global they've become."

"Very," he said, then smiled at her. "Have you had any interest in traveling?"

"Not a whole lot," she admitted. "I'm pretty much a homebody."

"Not a problem being a homebody, but sometimes people like to actually get out and leave so that they enjoy coming back."

She burst out laughing. "That's an odd reason to travel."

"I don't know," he said. "I think a lot of people travel like that. They just don't think about it that way. They all have to get away, but, as soon as they do, all they want to do is get home again."

"It just seemed funny, the way you put it," she said, shaking her head yet smiling.

He grinned. "That's good," he said. "Now let's go home."

"But we didn't get lunch."

"You know something? I can practically taste those ribs," he said. "And my instincts are saying, we need to get home."

She looked at him in surprise and then frowned. "Well, if that's what your instincts say," she said, "let's go."

He picked up the pace and headed home.

AS SOON AS they got close to town, Bonaparte slowed down. As they entered the town limits, he looked at her and asked, "Do you need anything from the office?"

She shook her head. "No."

He checked her again. "There haven't been any calls, have there?"

She shook her head and then quietly said, "No, and, yes, I noticed."

"Because there's no crime or because nobody's calling for help?"

"I honestly don't know," she said.

"Have you checked your radio?"

She looked at him in surprise and quickly pulled out her phone. "Run over to the station for me, will you?" Inside the station, she walked into her office and then headed to where the dispatch radios were. Nobody was in the office, but it also appeared that the radios weren't even working. She frowned, quickly pulled out her phone, and called Lana. "Hey, Lana. Were the phones working when you left yesterday?"

"Yes, of course they were," she said, her voice light, chirpy, and easily audible to Bonaparte.

"It just seems strange because there have been no calls at all today," Angela said.

"Well, there weren't any yesterday either," she said. "It's just really, really quiet."

At that, Angela stared at Bonaparte, one eyebrow raised. "Or they're not working."

Lana replied in an equally quiet voice, "Or you're just looking for trouble. It's a small town. We haven't had any problems in a long time. It used to be we had lots of weekends without trouble. Go home and rest, Sheriff. There are no problems."

Angela frowned, as she hung up the phone. She turned to him. "She doesn't seem to think there's a problem."

"Any way to check?"

"I'll call the township and have them check with 9-1-1 dispatch." It took her a few minutes, while he wandered around, studying the angles and anything to do with the office that he could, but it was all pretty well a common setup and otherwise empty. She turned and said, "Dispatch said that they've had phone problems for the last two days."

He nodded. "And has that been put down to anything?"

"They haven't found any cause for it."

"So, the true question is, ... do we have reason to be alarmed about it?"

"I guess not," she said, frowning. "It just seems odd."

"Have you heard rumors from anybody? Do the citizens know where you are, and would they try to find you, if they couldn't get through?"

"Well, if they knew where I was, they would certainly come find me," she said. "That's happened before, when the phones have been down. Or sometimes people just prefer to report their issues to me personally."

"So maybe it's not a case of there are no problems. Maybe it's a case of nobody wants to call you."

She frowned. "Why would that be?"

"Well, maybe it's not because they don't want to call you. What if it's because they're afraid they'll have some trouble if they do call you?"

She fisted her hands on her hips and glared at him. "Again you're talking in circles."

"I don't know what's behind it," he said. "But, if the phones are out, then that's a perfectly legitimate reason to worry," he said, "because that's obviously a problem. But, if nobody's calling, and they do actually need you, what are the chances they're not contacting you either because they don't want to cause trouble for you, or they don't want to be in trouble themselves?"

She ran a hand through her hair and stared at him. "I don't want to think that anybody here needs help but isn't calling."

"Do you have any people you normally check on?"

She nodded. "Some seniors I always keep an eye out

for."

"Have you heard from them lately?"

She shook her head. "No, but now you're making me worried," she said, groaning.

"And what about your girlfriend? The one who we spoke to. Would she tell you if there was a problem?"

"I don't know if she would now," she said. "Obviously we have a few issues we need to sort out."

"Not to mention potential charges."

She rolled her eyes at that. "That's just a great way to keep a friend, isn't it?"

"All I'm saying is, maybe you could check with her to see if she's heard of anything going on."

"Already on it," she said, with a sigh. "I just sent her a text. And this used to be such a nice simple town."

"I'm not sure that it isn't," he said. "Let's just be sure we haven't got any problems before they get there."

Her phone rang, and she answered and immediately frowned.

The conversation didn't appear to go too well. He looked over at her. She was frowning at him, as she spoke on the phone. "Look, Isabel. Is there a problem?"

He couldn't hear the other half of the conversation.

Angela replied, "Okay. I'm not sure what's going on, but I'm coming over." And, with that, she hung up. She looked over at him and said, "Let's go."

"I'm all good to go," he said, "but maybe you should tell me why."

"Because she sounded off, as in very off, like she couldn't talk."

"As in, she may have had unwanted company?"

She nodded slowly. "When I told her that I was coming

over, she told me to bring the cookies."

"Bring the cookies?"

"Yes, and the thing is, she has a gluten intolerance, and cookies aren't something she would eat."

"But she—" He stopped. "So it's a message?"

She nodded. "I would say so."

"Let's go then," he said. "Finally we might get to see some action."

Chapter 7

ANGELA INSISTED ON driving his truck, and the trip over to Isabel's place was fast and furious, but two blocks before her friend's street, Angela took a right turn and drove around.

"Where are we going?" Bonaparte asked.

"An alleyway stops two houses from her place," she said quietly. "There's also a walkway behind her place, but vehicles can't drive in there." She drove around the block, came up in the alleyway, parked there, and hopped out. She checked her weapon and then strolled to where the walkway started. He fell in step beside her. Up ahead she pointed to the house in question.

He nodded. "So somebody could certainly reach her place from back here. That doesn't sound very safe."

"Small town again. Remember?" she murmured.

He nodded. "Yeah, but you've got a bad apple here."

"I personally think," she said, "we have a couple of them. Maybe even a whole damn orchard." She gave him a cheeky smile and then said, "I'll go around to the front."

"Good," he said. "I'll search out the back and head in through that way."

"You might not like what you find," she said.

"You might not either," he said, by way of warning.

She frowned and nodded. She kept on walking, until

they came up to the side of the house. She pointed to the kitchen and then moved forward, so she could come around on the front side. As she walked closer to the house, she listened for any sounds, anything going on inside. Seemingly nobody was here. Still frowning, she walked until she got to the front walkway, where she stomped on the steps a little loud to let everyone know she was coming—but also to draw attention away from Bonaparte in the back. As she walked up onto the porch, she knocked on the door. There was no answer. She knocked again and then called out, "Isabel, where are you?"

The door opened, and Isabel was there, glaring at her. "I told you that I was fine."

Angela studied her friend intently, but she could see the nervous flicker in her eyes. "I know you did," she said, with a genial smile. "But that's what friends are for, isn't it? I just came to make sure you were okay, maybe have a cup of tea."

"I can't do tea right now," she said, but this time there was a tiny break in her voice. "It's not a good time."

"Well, I'm not so sure about that," she said. "Seems to me that we should sit down and talk. We've got a few issues. Remember that conversation from earlier?"

At that, her friend's face went blank and then flushed. "I really don't want to discuss it right now," Isabel said, and then gave her a meaningful smile and half a nudge toward the porch steps.

"I get it," Angela replied. She stepped forward, forcing her friend to step back again. "But I think these things need to be dealt with."

Just then Johnny stepped into view, stopping her forward progress. "Hey, bitch, she just said she doesn't want to talk with you now."

"Oh, look at that. Trouble. I see the riffraff found you," she said, with a glance at her friend to find a look of terror in her eyes. Angela studied Johnny. "You here alone?"

"What if I am?" he said. "I'm invited, but you're not. She told you to get lost."

"No, she didn't say that. She said, *it wasn't a good time.* That's a whole different story. *Not a good time* means that you're here. *Get lost* means she wants you here."

At that, Johnny's face flushed. "She wants me here just fine." He turned and glared at Isabel. "Don't you?"

She immediately nodded. "Of course I do."

At that, Angela just shook her head. "That's what this town has come to? Just threats and coercion?"

"Well, it's supposed to be *your* town," he said, with a sneer. "You're hardly a decent sheriff though, are you?"

"Well, that's all right," she said. "You know it takes a little bit of time to gather evidence for a case."

"You got no evidence. You got no case," he said immediately.

"Oh, but I'm not alone," she said. "We now have a team working on you guys."

"BS," he said flatly, his tone turning dark and ugly.

She looked at him and smiled. "Getting nervous, huh? That's probably a good thing. Maybe you just want to fly back home again to Daddy."

"I'm not going nowhere," he said. "This is where we need to be right now."

"And that's one of the things I don't quite get," she said. "What kind of deal are you running that makes you think that all the property here is worth something? You must know something nobody else does."

"I know a lot of things nobody else does," he said, the

sneer still evident in his tone. "You'll never know even half of what I know."

"Well, I don't mind that, since most of what you know is useless anyway," she murmured, her gaze going around the living room. "I still don't quite understand, but I'm sure the answers will come to light soon enough." She took another step into the living room. He immediately stepped forward, crossing his arms over his chest, and said, "You're not welcome here."

"Of course I am," she said. "Isabel and I have been good friends for a very long time."

"Well, we want some private time now," he said, "so get the hell out, bitch."

"And what if this is official police business? God knows I've got sufficient reason to sit here and to talk to her about some other issues."

"Then you better be bringing a team with you," he said, "because you're not welcome here, and we're not letting you in. So, go to the office and sit in your little room, where you think you're somebody."

"I don't think so," she replied.

At that, he reached for her, and, lightning quick, she grabbed his arm, bent him over double, and yanked his arm up behind his back, then pulled his feet out from under him, so he landed hard on the floor, face-first. Instantly she was on top of him, holding his arms backward.

"Get off me," he whined.

She pulled out her handcuffs and clipped them on. She looked over at Isabel. "Is it just him?"

Isabel immediately shook her head and pointed upstairs.

Angela nodded. "Go get me a zip tie, will you?"

Isabel immediately bolted into the kitchen, and then she

shrieked.

"That's okay. It's Bonaparte," Angela said. Isabel came back out, Bonaparte right behind her, with the zip ties. She looked at Bonaparte and pointed upstairs. He nodded and headed to the stairwell. She watched, as, instead of hopping up the stairs of the old house, he hopped onto the railing and casually made his way up, missing all the squeaking stairs.

"I didn't even get a chance to tell him that the fifth one's a doozy," Angela muttered, as she hopped up and made her way carefully up the stairs herself.

Isabel whispered at the bottom of the stairs, "What do I do?"

Angela looked at her friend and said, "Hide." Then Angela went up to the landing and around the corner, her weapon at the ready. By the time she got upstairs, Bonaparte was in a scuffle with a much smaller man. A much younger one. Once she reached them, Bonaparte already had the man subdued.

She looked at him and said, "Henry?"

Henry just glared at her.

"Who's the kid?" Bonaparte asked.

"This is Henry. I'm sure your dad will be thrilled to hear about your third strike."

"What strike?" he said. "I'm just here, visiting Isabel."

"I wonder if that's the story she'll tell when it comes to the courts?" she said.

"I didn't do anything. I'm just here visiting," he protested. "You got no right to even handcuff me."

"You think so?" she said. "I'm allowed to do all kinds of stuff."

"You better get your hands off me," he said. "You're done here anyway."

"Ah, so you've aligned yourself with them too, have you? That's okay," she said, with a shrug. "We'll see how you feel about it when they're in jail, and so are you."

There was only a tiny waver of his gaze. "They haven't done anything wrong," he said.

"Then what are you so worried about?" she asked. "If you haven't done anything wrong, why get all panicky and start issuing threats? If you're making threats, you'd better back them up."

And, with that, Bonaparte led him downstairs. She looked around, and, as she walked down with them, she asked Bonaparte, "Where was he anyway?"

"He was in the master bedroom."

She looked over at Isabel as she got to the bottom of the floor. "Why were they in your bedroom?"

"I don't know," Isabel said. "I really don't want to go back in there now."

"Come on up with me," she said. "Let's take a look and see if they stole anything."

"We're not thieves," Henry said from the floor. The other guy didn't say anything. "Jesus, you're so stupid," Henry told Angela, as he looked at the other man on the floor. "When he gets loose, he'll be so pissed at you."

"He might," she said, "but he's also likely to get pissed at you for letting your mouth run."

"He's not my boss," he said, with derision.

"Yeah?" She stopped on the stairs, looked at him, and said, "So you came here voluntarily, did you?"

"Of course I did," he said. "And Isabel let me in."

"That's funny because you know what? I got the impression she was afraid and in a very dangerous situation," she said. "And that sounds like kidnapping."

"Hell no," he said.

"And you were in her bedroom," she said, crossing her arms and leaning against the railing. "What the hell were you doing in there? Unless you had something nefarious on your mind."

He looked at her and then a look of horror appeared on his face. "That's just gross. She's old."

A strangled exclamation came from Isabel, but she managed to stay quiet.

"Ah, so rape wasn't part of your plan then?"

"God no," he said, "I already have a girlfriend. What do I need that for?"

"I don't know, but, when we find guys stalking women, and they're up in their bedrooms, nothing good comes to mind," she said. "However, we'll take your response under consideration."

BONAPARTE WATCHED THE interactions between her and the others. There was an obvious caring on her part, derision on the kid's part, and anger on Johnny's part. Bonaparte was still trying to figure out the other woman, Isabel. She had admitted that she and her mother had pulled some shenanigans to get her granddad's property sold, and, while Bonaparte understood their financial needs to cover escalating medical bills, the mother and the daughter had crossed a serious line.

He also didn't know what criminal action that entailed because it had apparently been the grandfather's wishes to sell his property. But, without a proper power of attorney, the other family members didn't have the legal right to do it. Bonaparte shook his head, thinking about all the times that there were actual crimes, wondering if this one was really something that mattered. It surely wasn't the priority at the moment because somehow these two idiots had latched on to Isabel, and that did matter.

He looked over at Angela. "Will you go up and check?"

"Yeah, are you okay to stay here with these two?"

He gave her a wolfish smile. "I'd be delighted to. Don't blame me, if you find them with broken noses or black eyes, when you come back down. They look like they might try to escape." She gave him an alarmed look, but he just gave her a sweet, almost angelic smile.

He meant it but would never cross the line like that. But he could hope that one of these two assholes wouldn't try to escape and cross the line for him. He would like nothing better than a chance to knock them both into tomorrow, and, from the look of these two, they realized it. The younger one shut up immediately, and the other one just lay on the floor, quiet. Bonaparte wondered at that and walked over and pulled out his ID.

Immediately he started screaming, "Don't you touch my wallet, you asshole."

Bonaparte gave him a hard nudge with his boot. "You were caught in the criminal act of threatening an officer of the law, so I have full authority to check your ID." He pulled it out and realized a fair bit of identification was inside—all in his name. Bonaparte walked over to the table and quickly laid them all out and took photos. He was just behind both of the men's backs, so they couldn't see what he was doing.

He checked the rest and found nothing of interest except a note, a little piece of paper, with a series of numbers, like a phone number. He quickly took a photo of that too. He sent it to Levi. Bonaparte's best guess was that this was probably

Daddy Gapone's untraceable number, but Levi would confirm that later. Johnny also had several thousand dollars on him. Bonaparte whistled at that. "Wow, think you're rich, huh?" He put all the IDs back inside the wallet and walked over to pop it into the guy's back pocket.

"If that money is missing," he said, "I'll have your badge."

"I don't really care," he said. "Rich assholes like you are no threat to me." The guy just glared, but he was powerless to do anything. Bonaparte grabbed the guy's phone next, where he flicked through his Contacts. Bonaparte noted a few before handing it back.

Walking over to Henry, the second guy, Bonaparte went through the same process. This one didn't even bother to protest. But, then again, there wasn't much in his possession. When Bonaparte was finished, he put the wallet back in the kid's pocket. As soon as Angela came back down, he could tell something was wrong by the odd expression on her face.

Immediately the two men started yelling and complaining about Bonaparte to Angela. She looked at him, one eyebrow raised. He shrugged and said, "I've got copies of their IDs. We'll need to figure out what's going on here."

"Nothing's going on," Isabel said, quietly at her side.

He looked at her and smiled. "So you won't mind showing me your ID then."

She was startled and immediately turned to Angela. "Angela's known me all her life."

"Then you won't object to me taking a look inside your wallet then, will you?"

Isabel hesitated, and he wondered at that and tilted his head to look at her inquiringly. She looked back at the other two men and over at him and then back at Angela. Isabel gave a small headshake, which shot Angela's eyebrows straight up. Then Isabel said, "Fine."

Bonaparte took a quick look at her ID and photographed it, before handing it back to her.

Angela motioned to Bonaparte. "We need to take these two into the station." He nodded, then walked over, picked up the one by the shirt and put him on his feet. Bonaparte did it so fast and in such a smooth move that the guy didn't have a chance to do anything but squawk. Bonaparte did the same with the second one, then led them out to the truck, where he buckled them into the back seat. He turned on the engine and waited for Angela to join him.

He watched the two women, discussing something on the front steps. Judging by their body language, they were both definitely unhappy. He wished he'd had a chance to check into Isabel's background, but instead he texted her DL now to Levi. She was connected to these two losers, so Angela's best friend was now a whole different story. Angela hopped into the truck, and they drove back to the station.

"I want a lawyer," the one man said.

She nodded. "You'll get yours," she said. "In the meantime you can park your butt in jail, until I can sort out the paperwork."

"I don't want to go to jail," Henry sniveled.

"Well, that's where you're headed, and, at the rate you're going, you could be there on a permanent basis," Bonaparte said in exasperation. "These guys you've signed up with are bad news, so that's what you get."

Henry went quiet at that. But intermittent checks in the rearview mirror revealed a young man who kept looking over at the other guy, clearly wondering if Johnny would say something to get them out of this. Little did the kid know that he was just roadkill, as far as these guys were concerned. A lot of people used young punks, like Henry, to build themselves up. Having somebody on hand to push around and to bark orders at made people like Johnny feel like they were doing something special. They just used these kids for information and for local access. And that's likely what this was all about.

All Bonaparte knew for sure was that something was going on here, and it was likely about the properties, since that's what these brothers were well-known for. So why didn't anybody know more about it? As soon as they got to the station, he marched the two guys inside the office and waited at her side for Angela to do the paperwork.

That was something he couldn't really help her with, unless she asked him to and provided some information. So, in the meantime, he sent a message to Levi, asking for info on any local councilmen on the boards for the town's property development or at the county level or any connection like that which could explain why these guys were all over the locals. As far as Bonaparte was concerned, something had to be going through, something being approved, or something that nobody else knew about.

Levi immediately called him back. "That's a hell of a thought," he said on the phone. "And a good one."

Taking several steps back into another room, Bonaparte spoke in a quiet voice, keeping an eye on the prisoners all the while. "Well, somebody knows something, and they're trying to get a jump on it, before anybody else finds out."

"But that also could mean that it's not been approved."

"It could even be that it hasn't come up for approval yet. If they're playing a long game, it could be something that they know will go through eventually, but they're taking a chance and buying up quite a bit of property in town here."

"So, like a highway?"

"That would be my thought."

"I'll get on it," Levi said, "and see what our underground network can come up with. Also the tax man is already looking at Ronnie's and Johnny's IRS returns. The brothers own multiple real estate holdings under various holding companies. We're still on it, but it'll take a pro to get to the bottom of this, shifting through all the layers, trying to hide the ultimate owner."

Finished on the phone, Bonaparte walked back to where the two guys sat. He smiled at them. "Comfortable?"

The young kid looked at him and said, "I have to go the bathroom."

"I can do that," he said. He went to lift him up, but the guy hopped to his feet.

"Get your hands off me."

"Okay," he said, "guess you're not going to the bathroom."

"I have to go," he said.

"Well then, you need to walk to the bathroom," he said. "I'm not carrying you."

"You would touch me."

"I would help you get on your feet," he said. "But, hey, if you're one of those guys, then whatever."

At that, Henry stopped and stared at him. "What do you mean, *one of those guys?*"

Bonaparte gave him a blank look. "The washroom's down here. You have to go or not?"

"But you have to untie my hands first."

"I'll untie your hands *when* you get into the washroom," he said. "And, if you're going to pull something, you might as well talk yourself out of that right now."

"Why? Because you're such a big tough guy? You're just big," he said. "You're nothing beyond that."

Bonaparte smiled and said, "So, bathroom or not?" He used a deliberately bored voice to let the kid know that he was about to get all the time he wanted because Bonaparte would walk away and no way would he walk back to the kid anytime soon.

"Fine, bathroom," the kid said resentfully.

Bonaparte walked him to the bathroom, opened up the door, and checked inside to be sure it was safe and secure. Unclipping the handcuffs, he put the kid inside. Then Bonaparte just stood at the open door.

"Close the door!" Henry griped.

"Too bad, kid. When you're in jail, you'll be in full view of everybody," he said. "So you might as well get down to business."

The kid just looked at him, glanced at the door, then turned and walked over to the urinal. "You just want to watch."

"Yeah, that's probably your deal, not mine."

"Jesus, what an asshole," Henry muttered. Bonaparte heard him urinating and waited for the kid to finish washing his hands, before stepping back to the doorway. The kid came back out toward the doorway, but it was obvious he was looking for anywhere to run. Bonaparte immediately grabbed him by the shoulder and got him handcuffed again.

"You don't have to handcuff me, you know?" Henry whined.

"You were checking out your exits," he said, "so you earned no trust on my part." The kid just glared at him. Bonaparte walked him over and sat him on the other side of the room from where Johnny was.

"Why can't I sit over there?" he asked.

"I don't want you two talking, getting your stories straight."

"You don't know anything about it," he muttered.

"Yeah? Well, you might be surprised."

As soon as Angela came back out, she looked at Johnny and said, "Your lawyer's on the way."

He nodded. "Of course. That's what I pay him for."

He spoke in that bored and entitled rich man's tone that made Bonaparte just want to punch him in the face. He walked over to Angela, stepped into her office, and said, "Do we have anything?"

"Well, we've got a few things," she said. "But nothing that'll hold them."

"Can't we hold them long enough so he at least has to see the judge?"

"Yep, I can do that," she said, "and that'll be Monday."

"Will we have the ballistics results back by then?"

Chapter 8

ANGELA LOOKED UP at Bonaparte in shock. "Yeah, no," she said, with a headshake. "And that's a hard no."

"Right," he said, then shook his head. "I keep forgetting we have to play by the standard law enforcement rules, regulations, and departments."

"We sure do," she said cheerfully. "But that doesn't necessarily mean that Johnny'll get to walk."

"It sure sounds like it to me."

"What I need," she said, "is to talk to Isabel."

He thought about that and nodded. "Right. Any chance of getting her to testify?"

"I'm not sure," Angela said. "It depends how afraid she is about what she's done."

"You think they'll still hold that over her?"

"Well, if you had good leverage like that, wouldn't you?"

"Yep," he said, "definitely."

"Then you know what her answer is." Angela smiled and said, "But I definitely need to talk to her. Who knows what all these guys have said and done, but they've clearly put the fear of God in her."

"If not, somebody else will be there soon." He looked at her and said, "Shall we go pick her up?"

"I just called her to come in, and she refused."

"Then we need to have another in-person talk."

"Yep. I was thinking we could just lock up these two and drive right back over again."

"Sounds good." He marched the two men into the jail cells and watched with quiet satisfaction as the sheriff locked them up.

When she tucked away the key, she said, "Come on. Let's go."

"What about my lawyer?" Johnny called out.

"Office hours are closed," Angela said. "You'll talk to him Monday." And, with that, she closed the basement door with a definitive *click*.

Bonaparte stared at her, with a look of absolute delight. "Oh, I do like that."

She winked at him. "I will have to come back and feed them later," she said, "and they do have a urinal in there. But, other than that, they're good to go until Monday morning." In the distance she could hear them hollering. "It's a trick we've often pulled," she said, with a chuckle. "It all depends on what problems we have with people on whether we let them out fast or not."

"Yeah," he said, "I understand fully." They quickly got into his vehicle, Angela was driving once more, and she went back to Isabel's place.

As they got out, he looked up and frowned. "Doesn't look like anybody's home."

Angela started to swear. "I sure hope she hasn't run."

"And, if she did, where would Isabel go?"

"I don't know, but it would be the worst thing she could do." Angela raced to the door and found it open. She called out, "Isabel?" But heard nothing except a weird empty hollowness.

He swore and raced to the backyard, just as he heard a

vehicle firing up. He bolted through the alleyway path to find Isabel pulling out from there. He opened the passenger door, scaring her. She shrieked, and he hopped inside and sat there.

She looked at him, wild-eyed. "No, no, no, no!" she said. "I have to leave. You don't understand. I have to leave now!"

"I know that you're involved a whole lot more than you're willing to tell your friend—your friend who's gone to bat for you," he said in a hard voice. "And you were just gonna bail on her, and that'll never sit well with me."

Isabel glared at him. "You don't understand."

"I know you're in trouble," he said. "I understand that part really well."

"But you don't know how much trouble," she said, "and these guys are not fun to deal with."

"And, since you've already committed a crime, they're leveraging it against you, right?"

She nodded, sick, her expression revealing the level of stress she'd been under. "I didn't do anything other than what my grandfather wanted," she said. "It's not fair."

"And who else was involved?"

"My mom," she said, "but we were both the recipients in the will anyway."

"So, you just slightly jumped it forward and went ahead with the property sale."

"We didn't do anything wrong."

"No, maybe not," he said, "but it's a fine line, isn't it? Because, if Granddad had died, you would have just dealt with the courts."

"And who needed that?" she cried out.

"Regardless of your bravado, you obviously feel like what

you did was wrong because you keep falling into their blackmail schemes."

She stared at him in shock, and then her shoulders sagged, and she nodded. "That's it, isn't it?"

"It absolutely is," he said quietly. "And, once you fall into that trap, and they've got something on you, then you're hooked. And so are they. Because now you're somebody that they can wield as they need to. The question really is, how far are you willing to go, and how many other people in this town have they got in the same position?"

She slowly shook her head. "I didn't even think of it that way," she said, bewildered. "I've never done anything like that."

"No, but you were trying to rush through something that your grandfather wanted anyway and that he had worked hard to get and that he needed for his care and your mother's treatments, correct? So it makes sense that you were also confused and dealing with a lot of stress."

"Yes, and you make it sound so reasonable," she said, "but five minutes ago you made it sound like I was the worst criminal ever."

"No," he said, "that wasn't me, that was you already thinking you were. That's how people get you caught up in guilt like that."

"And what am I supposed to do now?" she asked.

"You come and face the music, and, with any luck, your friend can get you off, particularly if you help her with this case."

She stared at him in shock and then slowly said, "No, no, no, no. You really don't understand. These guys play for real."

"So do the courts of law," he said.

Her face twisted up. "Now you're doing exactly what they were doing."

"Except that I actually understand the law," he said. "They were just trying to manipulate you for totally selfish reasons."

"So are you," she said mutinously.

He laughed. "Good," he said, "that's what you should be saying. But the fact of the matter is, you already know you've done wrong and that there will be repercussions. Whether they're light or heavy will depend on your actions right now."

She opened her mouth and closed it several times. "I should never have done it," she whispered.

And, with that, Angela arrived. She looked at her friend, disappointment on her face. "Were you really trying to run?"

Isabel looked at her and burst into tears. "You don't know what these people are like," she blubbered.

"No," she said, "but I've known many like them." She opened the door and motioned her friend back out of the vehicle.

"They'll kill me," Isabel said in a flat voice.

"Well, I hope not," she said. "So tell me. How did these guys find out what you did in the first place?"

"I don't know. They must have somebody at the nursing home or something," she said, her shoulders sagging. "Somebody must have overheard the two of us."

"Or they guessed," Bonaparte said quietly. "People like that prey on people like you, and they can see when you've done something wrong because you act guilty."

"Well, I probably did then, yeah," she said. "It's been a tough load to haul."

"I'm sure it has been," Angela said. She led her friend

back into the house.

Bonaparte watched the area as they headed back inside. He had that feeling of being watched. He asked Angela, "Are you taking her back to the station?"

"I should," she said. "We need to have a talk with her, and obviously she's too spooked to be left on her own."

"No," Isabel said, "I'll stay."

"I can't trust you on that," Angela said firmly. "So back to the station we go." She looked over at Bonaparte. "Why?

He stepped forward, and, in a low voice that Isabel couldn't hear, he said, "We're being watched."

"Of course we are," she said. "What do you want to do about it?"

"I'll go for a walk," he said, with a grin. "Take her back. I'll meet you there."

"You don't want a ride?"

"Nope, I know the town enough by now." He added, "I'll get there without any problem."

She nodded, escorted Isabel into the front seat of his truck. Looking at Bonaparte, she asked, "Hey, would you mind moving her car back?"

He looked back at the vehicle and said, "Sure, I can do that."

She watched for a moment, then hopped in.

"Who is that guy?" Isabel asked quietly.

"You met him before. He's my new deputy," she said.

"Well, he's not like any of the others, and he doesn't act the same."

"Nope," she said. "He's an entirely different animal. But I needed backup. Too much crap going on here right now, and, like you said, these guys are something else."

"You don't even know all of it," she said. "They threatened to kill Mom."

"And they probably went to her and threatened to kill you too," she said. "Did you even talk to your mom about it?"

"I didn't want her to know that we could be in deep trouble."

"The deep trouble you're talking about is probably one that these guys created," she said.

"What do you mean?"

"They bought the property, didn't they?"

"Well sure, and they put us into that position of having to hurry, or we'd lose the deal. They kept dropping the offer. We waited for the lawyer to get the power of attorney, but—"

"But your grandfather wasn't cognizant enough to do that either, was he?"

She slowly shook her head. "No, and it was their idea," she whispered.

"And now they've got you, don't they? You didn't tell me that. You just said maybe they had someone there who overheard."

"Well, they weren't there at the time," she said, "but, yeah, they put the idea in our heads, and then they just stuck around and mentioned a couple things that just kept our minds going in that direction," she said in frustration. "How could we be so gullible?"

"Because it's what you wanted, so you were looking for a way to make it happen," she said.

Isabel fell silent, as they drove toward the station. "What'll happen to me?"

"I'm not sure. I'll talk to the prosecutor and see what we have for a case."

"A case?" she said bitterly. "You could just let me go."

"I could, but then I wouldn't be upholding the law. And you'd be the first one to slam me for it, if you weren't sitting there on the opposite side of the law."

"But it is me. I am sitting right here. I can't go to jail."

"I hear you, and I understand that, and I get that you wish you'd thought about that early on. But, in the meantime, we have to discuss it and see what's going on and see if you'll help with this problem or not. Although you've lied to me so many times, I'm not sure if you would help or hurt the case at this point."

"If I help, I'll get an easier sentence?"

"I can't promise that," she said carefully. "Jail may or may not be a part of it. I can't tell you anything with certainty at this point. I know that it's a dubious area. Everybody knew the property was for sale for a while and that your family was under some pressure. But that won't necessarily let you off the hook completely."

"Community service sounds nice," she said, with a heavy sigh.

"And I will mention that," she said, looking over at her friend of many, many years. "I just can't let you walk."

"Of course not, you're much too moral."

"And why did you elect me?" Angela asked.

"Because I knew you couldn't be bribed," she said in frustration. "But I wasn't expecting to be the one needing to bribe you."

At that, Angela burst out laughing. "That's a good thing then," she said. "Because you didn't see yourself heading down this life of crime."

"God, no," she murmured. "I was never heading in this direction. I was always the Goody Two-Shoes."

"Maybe. So what did those two say to you at your house?" she said, abruptly changing the subject.

"They told me to smarten up and to not talk."

"Or?"

"Or my mother would have an accident," she said bitterly.

"And do you think they went to your mother and told her the same thing?"

"Probably," she said.

"Call her."

Isabel looked at her hesitantly. "I didn't want to open that can of worms."

"Really? And who would you call when you went to jail?"

"Well, that's harsh," she said.

"Sure it is," Angela said, with a heavy sigh, not knowing what her friend would have to face. She didn't think it would be a hard sentence, but sometimes, you know, in this very conservative area, things got a little more difficult than anybody expected. She pulled into the station, hopped out, and said, "Come on inside."

"What if I don't?" her friend Isabel said, with a moment of bravado.

"Then you run, and I come after you, and then you *really* get thrown in jail for evading arrest," she said. "If you do manage to get out of the town and out of the state," she said, "then we go across country, looking for you. Then you spend your life looking over your shoulder, while you wait to see how long it takes me to catch you."

"Wow," Isabel muttered, as she walked toward the station. "You didn't put it very nicely."

"You were already caught leaving your garage in your

car. What did you think would happen?"

"I guess I'm not really built for a life of crime, am I?"

"Nope, it takes a certain kind of person to make it happen. Somebody who's willing to pay the price of their conscience and their soul in order to make it do what they want it to do," she said. "That's never been you."

"Well, remember that when the judge, … well, when you're in a position to put in a good word for me."

"Oh, I'll remember," she said. "I won't willfully throw you away and lose the key, without even trying to get you a better resolution. But first things first, and that means you have to fess up to what you did, why you did it, what the factors were that affected your decision. And that means the manipulation from these guys too. And then what happened afterward."

"Oh, is that all you want?" Isabel asked sarcastically.

"Well, it's a hell of a good place to start," Angela said. "We can't afford to let these guys go wild on the streets, creating all kinds of chaos."

"What about your other deputies?" she asked suddenly.

"You know what happened to them. They were warned to stay away from me."

"And they listened."

"Well, wouldn't you? You already kept all this stuff from me."

"I couldn't tell you," she said, "because I'd already done wrong myself."

"And, once you start down that path, you alienate so many people," Angela said, "and that makes life a hell of a lot more difficult for you. And everybody else."

"Yeah, well, I had no way of knowing that ahead of time. I've never done anything like this before."

"And that is something that will go in your favor too," she said quietly. Angela sagged, as they walked through the station. She motioned at a chair that sat by a small empty table and brought over a pad of paper and a pen. "Go ahead and write it out."

"You know that, if I had a laptop or a computer, I could do it a lot faster."

"Well, you don't," she said, "and I'm not giving you access to anything connected to the internet, and everything here is connected."

Isabel just stared at her. "That's hardly fair."

"No way, you already tried to run once. I can't have you contacting anybody," she said. "So sit and make your statement. Then I'll figure out what I'm doing next, but the statement has to get done first."

Angela stared at her friend, as Isabel bowed her head to the page in front of her, because Angela really didn't know what she would do with this mess. This was the first time she'd ever been put in this spot. Even after all the years she'd been the sheriff here, and knowing all the problems associated with policing her friends and neighbors in a small area, but this one seemed like the worst.

Angela understood exactly why Isabel did what she did, but she'd also put herself in a position where she could get in trouble and be leveraged to help these other assholes. And they were bad news for everybody. So Isabel didn't just do something for herself, she did something against everyone else, and that would be hard to forgive.

With a shake of her head, Angela walked to the jail area to check on her two prisoners and stood there in shock, when she realized the jail was empty.

Both men were gone.

BONAPARTE WALKED AROUND the area, trying to flush out whoever was watching him. He hadn't seen who it was, it was just that feeling, that nagging sensation in the back of his mind and at the back of his neck. When his phone rang, he looked down to see it was Angela. "You miss me already?"

"Both men are gone from the jail cells," she said.

He froze. "Shit," he murmured.

"Yeah, that's one word for it. I've definitely got a problem now."

"Well, we have two escaped convicts," he said, turning to look around. "I wonder if that's why I've still got that feeling of being watched."

"Well, now you really need to watch your back," she said, "because both are dangerous. Henry, because he's just so young and stupid, and Johnny, because he'll want to get back at you."

"Yeah, I got it," he said. "I'm headed your way. Can you determine how they got out?"

"Afraid so," she said bitterly. "It looks like a key." And, with that, she hung up.

He looked down at the phone in his hand and shook his head. She really was dealing with a regular shitstorm. As he walked, his phone rang, and he checked it, glad to see it was Levi. Bonaparte quickly filled him in on all the events of the day so far. Even as Levi started swearing, Bonaparte said, "I'm headed back to the station right now. I'm about ten minutes out."

"I'd get there a little faster, if you can, because there's no guarantee that she wasn't being set up for somebody still in that station."

He winced at that. "Well, she is armed."

"Which won't make a damn bit of difference if they take her by surprise."

And Bonaparte knew that was true. "Well, we've also got Isabel in there too."

"Yeah, and I know that's her friend, but we don't know what kind of a friend she'll be when push comes to shove."

"Especially now," Bonaparte said and explained what had happened with her.

"Wow, these guys are good. They find victims all over the place, apply pressure, and individually they all crumble. And, next thing you know, there is a willing army, available to do whatever is needed to keep themselves out of jail."

"Well, if you think about it, it's not all that stupid of an idea. And it seems to be effective."

"Yep. I also checked in with the planning committee. Apparently they're in the process of approving a major highway change that will go right through her town."

"Aah," he said, with a smile. "That's exactly what I wanted to hear."

"You think that's why they're doing this?"

"Absolutely. A lot of money to be made. Malls, gas stations, etcetera. Whatever else the government is looking to appropriate for the highway."

"Well, there's your motive then, at least for now," Levi said. "And, of course, they're on hand."

"Yep, because," Bonaparte said, "and you probably don't know this, but the town has an ordinance, where you sell to the townsfolk first. Before you sell to a stranger."

"So, by being in place, they're actually getting a chance to purchase properties ahead of anybody else."

"Yes," Bonaparte said. "And then, because it hasn't been approved yet, developers have been sniffing around, but nothing's really sold. So the brothers are getting set up to earn a quick buck by flipping the properties."

"Every damn one of them," Levi said. "Now hustle over there."

As Bonaparte loped through town, heading for the sheriff's station, he wondered just how much money was at stake. When he figured the size of the highway, the destinations that could be reached by going this way, he realized it would be a lot. It would involve gas stations and fast-food chains. It could be a whole new development that would go up. Even if they did nothing but flip it, the badass brothers would still make a sizable profit. And that included other properties as well.

He frowned at that, thinking about what would become of Angela's acreage. That was one of the bigger tracts. He quickly texted Levi back and asked where Angela's property was situated in terms of that new highway. Bonaparte got a response, saying Levi would check, then pocketed his phone. Bonaparte realized chances were good it would be right smack in the middle of Angela's land.

She was in the middle of this mess, and that meant her property probably was as well. And, if they took her out, it would make a massive difference in income level for the brothers. Bonaparte swore, as he thought about the level of risk, and he picked up the pace. He didn't know what the hell was going on, but Angela was at risk, and it looked like that wouldn't change anytime soon.

Chapter 9

NSIDE THE STATION, Angela put on a pot of coffee, as Isabel wrote out her statement. Angela hadn't told her friend that the two men holding her hostage in her home had been in jail and that now they were both gone. But Angela had been checking the station thoroughly, including inside closets, the washrooms, under desks, everywhere. It appeared that they just unlocked the damn gate and walked right out the front door. She checked the security cameras and found the system had been completely disabled. She started to swear then. She sat down and fired off an email to one of the other sheriffs, with a photo of both men. Then she contacted the sheriff on the other side. Both responded right away.

One called her and said, "Wow, you've got a real problem there, don't you?"

"Yeah," she said. "And it looks like one of my deputies helped them get out."

"But you don't know that for sure, do you?"

"No, not yet," she said, "because, of course, they disabled the security cameras."

There was silence on the other end for a moment, then he spoke. "Did you call up more deputies?"

"I have one right now," she said.

"What about getting a second one?"

"Well, this one is the size of two," she joked. But inside she knew it was no joking matter and said, "Just keep an eye out for these guys, will you?"

"I'm pretty sure they've just gone home, all cocky and sure of themselves. Will you pick them up?"

"I will," she said, "but, if I can't hold them, it just becomes a running joke."

"It does at that," he said. "Getting those locks changed is pretty rough though."

"No, I got a big padlock," she said. "I'll use that instead. I'm just waiting for my deputy to return, and I've also got somebody writing up a statement right now," she said. "I can't leave right away."

He swore. "Look. If you want me to come over, I will."

"And I might need you to," she said, "so thanks for the offer. I appreciate it very much. I'll let you know what happens in the next little bit." When she hung up from that call, she rose and poured herself a cup of coffee and asked Isabel if she wanted one.

Isabel looked up from her table with a frown and then nodded. "Yes, please."

Angela poured two cups, dropping off Isabel's, and walked back to her office, then checked to see where Bonaparte was. She stared out the window but kept out of any direct line of fire. It was just one of those conversations in her head that she knew would not have a good answer. If these guys had any idea that they could shoot her here, then chances were they probably would. They would love the irony of the sheriff being murdered in her own station. When she caught sight of movement outside, she looked over to see Bonaparte heading quickly toward her. She smiled as she watched his huge frame lope toward her easily.

It surprised her, given his size.

He came up the front steps in two bounds. "Any more trouble?"

"No," she said quietly, "and I did find a large padlock."

"Good," he said. "You want me to go pick them up again?"

She hesitated and then nodded. "Are you up for it?"

He gave her a feral grin. "Are you kidding? I'm just waiting for the chance."

"It might get ugly."

"Even better," he said.

She smiled. "I don't feel like you should go alone."

"But that's what I'm here for," he said, "and you can't leave her."

"No," she said, frowning at her friend. "She's writing up a statement right now."

"Good. It might not be enough, but still it's good to get it done," he murmured.

She knew exactly what he meant. "Go pick them up," she said, "and let's just hope they won't give you any guff over it all."

"They will," he said cheerfully. "Not to worry though. I've got this."

After giving him the address, she watched as he hopped into the truck and took off. As she went back inside, she watched Isabel stare at her curiously.

"What was that all about?"

She stared back and said, "Police business."

Isabel flushed. "I guess I deserved that."

"I don't know what to do now," Angela said. "We were friends, until this."

"We still are friends," Isabel said. "I crossed the line, I

know, but I'm not really any different than I ever was before."

"I hope not," Angela said, as she studied her face. "There could be some tough questions and answers coming up."

She nodded. "I know, but I do realize what I've done wrong."

"And yet you're not willing to talk to your mother?"

She winced. "I can," she said hesitantly.

Just then came a cry from the front door. "Isabel, is that you?"

Angela looked over at Isabel and said, "Looks like the news has already traveled. You may have failed to mention that your sister was in the middle of all this too?"

And, at that, Lana hopped into the station, looked at her sister, and asked, "What happened?"

"What do you mean, *what happened?*" Isabel said drily. "Have Henry and Johnny or other guys been bothering you?" As the color washed out of her sister's face, Isabel said, "They have, haven't they?"

She nodded. "Ever since the nursing home, getting Granddad's signature," she said, sagging onto a nearby chair but looking sideways at Isabel.

"Oh, my God," Isabel said, "me and Mom didn't even really think about it. We were just so panicked, trying to get the sale done, before Granddad got even worse."

"And that's what you need to tell a judge," Angela said.

Lana stared at her, looked at her sister, and said, "Judge?" Her word came out with a squeak.

Isabel looked sad and nodded. "Yeah, you know what we did was wrong."

"Maybe, but it wasn't criminal," Lana said. The two women looked at her, and Lana slowly sagged in place. "Oh, my God," she said, "that's what you think? It is, isn't it?"

"You forged a signature on a legal document," Angela said, "when you could have just gotten a lawyer to deal with it."

"We couldn't have done anything," Lana said. "Granddad was right there—well, as much as he ever was. It's not like we forged it."

"It's exactly like you forged it. The bottom line is, it's still something that has to be discussed," Angela said. "And that puts you and your sister in the position you find yourself in right now. And then we have the actions of these men. Did those two brothers or others ever approach you afterward?"

Lana tried to look surprised and failed miserably, then sagged even further in her chair. She looked over at her sister. "Did they approach you?"

Isabel said, "Of course they did. Constantly."

"What were you supposed to do for them?" Lana asked Isabel.

"Get close to Angela and find out what was going on." Isabel looked over at Angela and said, "But I didn't do that, I swear."

Angela shrugged. "I wouldn't have let you," she said quietly.

"I told them that too," Isabel said.

Angela looked straight at Isabel. "Too bad you didn't mention your sister's involvement. That changes things considerably." She looked at Lana. "So what about you? What did they want you to do?"

She flushed and remained silent.

"Ah," Angela said. "Weren't you dating Deputy Johnson at one time?"

At that, Lana's face turned bright red. "Yes," she said.

"But she broke up with him ages ago," Isabel said.

Lana was silent, looking at the floor.

"So did you suddenly become inspired to reconcile?" Angela asked her.

Lana looked like she wanted to disappear.

"Does he know that you took the key from his pocket? The key he was supposed to return and didn't?"

At that, Lana's face went from red to pure white.

"Oh, my God," Angela said. "So it was you who walked into the jail and let two prisoners go free."

Isabel looked at her in confusion and back at Lana. "What are you talking about?"

"Henry and Johnny are both missing from the jail downstairs," Angela said, "and your sister's the one who let them out."

Isabel looked at her sister in horror. "Do you know they were in my house and kept me kidnapped inside? And that is where I would likely still be if Angela hadn't come to rescue me?"

Lana stared at her in shock. "No, I didn't know anything about that," she cried out. She stared at Angela. "What have I done?"

"Well, on top of the forgery, you've now aided and abetted two criminals in a successful escape from custody," Angela said, shaking her head at the stupidity of these women. "I can't get you two out of this mess that you've created all by yourselves." She turned to her best friend. "Good God, Isabel. If you'd told me that Lana was involved, I might have headed some of this off."

"But, but ..." Lana sputtered, "that's not what I meant to do."

"Where did they go?" Angela asked, stepping forward and glaring at Lana.

Lana shrank back. "I don't know," she said. "I didn't have a choice."

"And does Deputy Johnson know about this?"

Lana glanced at her and then away, without speaking.

"Damn it, Lana," Angela said, "silence only digs you deeper into this hole. Start talking and don't you dare lie to me."

Shamefaced, Lana slowly nodded. "He knew he was supposed to return the keys, but the brothers found out and told him not to, in case they might come in handy some time."

"Or did he get a copy made?" Angela asked in a hard voice.

"He tried," she rushed to say, "but nobody here would do it, and, when he tried to take them into town, they wouldn't do it there either."

"That's because they're not allowed to," she said, "because they are supposed to be secure. Something Deputy Frank Johnson knows very well. But I'm sure, with enough poking and prodding, with enough money and threats, somebody would have eventually," she said bitterly.

She pulled out her phone and phoned Bonaparte. "Watch out for those two," she said. "Isabel failed to mention that her sister, Lana, was in the middle of the forgery mess as well. It would have been nice to know because her lack of judgment and questionable morals made her an obviously easy target to do just about anything. Apparently the brothers blackmailed Lana, who is currently sitting in front of me now, into reconciling with her boyfriend, the soon-to-be ex-Deputy Johnson. He was supposed to return his keys, of course, but chose not to after willingly attempting to get them copied. Anyway, Lana used them to walk into the jail and to let go the very same prisoners who were terrorizing her sister earlier today, so the brothers could spread more havoc on our community."

There was silence on the other end.

Angela reached up, rubbed her temple, and said, "Yes, I know. This is Peyton Place. Drama surrounds these guys."

"Good," he said, "I'll have even more fun pulling them in then."

"If you think it's safe," she murmured.

"I ought to be safe enough," he said. "Believe me. At this point in time, I'm really hoping they do something stupid."

"But you're alone, and you have no backup."

"Nope, I don't. You just get that jail cell ready. I'll have two bodies ready to warm those seats back up in no time."

She hung up, looked over Lana and Isabel, and said, "Where's your mother?"

"She's at home. Why?"

"Because I'm not sure I can let you two go home."

"She has—you have to," Lana said, jumping to her feet, staring at her in shock. "Mama has no one else."

"And now Mama will have to go to the seniors' home for care by somebody who *can* look after her."

Both women stared at her in horror.

"Did either of you even think about Mama," Angela said, "when you started your life of crime and then buckled under the brothers' blackmail? Did you even consider what would happen to Mama?"

Both women just looked at each other, tears welling up, and they shook their heads.

"Jesus," Angela said, staring ahead. "I'll go call the prosecutor."

"Please, please, please," Lana said, "you have to let me go home."

"Why? I can't trust you to actually go home, even to take care of your mother. When I left dear Isabel here on her own, she had already packed up her car and was leaving town."

Lana turned to stare at Isabel. "What!"

Isabel flushed. "I didn't know what else to do," she said. "I was terrified. I knew those men would come back. I knew they'd get out of jail one way or another, though it didn't occur to me that my own sister would help them escape, but I knew they'd be coming back after me."

"And what about me?" Lana asked, staring at her sister in shock. "Were you just leaving me with Mama and Granddad to worry about?"

"Only until I could figure out what to do," she said. "I had to get away. You weren't the one being held hostage in your house," she said.

"And it was Henry and Johnny," Angela said, looking at Lana. "Who did you deal with?"

Lana's face turned red and then white and then red again. Finally she admitted, "It was Ronnie."

"No surprise there," Angela said. She walked over, grabbed another pad of paper and a pen, and dropped them in front of Lana and said, "Start writing down everything that happened." The woman looked up at her and said, "Can't I use a laptop or something?"

"No," Angela said, rolling her eyes. "You can't. I'm sure you remember how to print at least, if you don't remember how to write." And, with that, Angela stepped through to the back, where the women couldn't hear her, and yet

Angela could still keep an eye on everything and called the prosecutor.

When he answered the phone, his voice was hard and fed up. "I'm enjoying a Saturday afternoon with my family," he said. "Why are you disturbing me?"

"Because I've got a problem, sir," she said quietly, and she quickly laid out the problems.

"Good Lord," he said, "is this all related to your deputies quitting?"

"Yes," she said, "we've got a group forcibly trying to buy up property in town. I'm not yet exactly sure why, but I'm certain there is a compelling reason. Now I have two sisters who got caught doing something they shouldn't have, who've been blackmailed and threatened, and one of them actually released my prisoners from my jail."

He groaned, and then he laughed, and afterward he cried out, "Good God. That's just too ridiculous to believe."

"I know," she said. "I've got them both writing up statements, while I'm sitting here, keeping an eye on them."

"And you have no deputies left?"

"None of my original crew, but I have one on loan," she said. "It is my belief that my former deputies may have been subject to threats as well, but I have no proof of that. At the moment, what I need to nail down is what charges I can bring up on these two women, though it's complicated by the fact that their mother is undergoing cancer treatment at home, and their grandfather is in a care facility with Alzheimer's."

He coughed into the phone. "And they didn't think about that first?"

"It doesn't seem that they thought about very much," she said quietly.

He sighed heavily. "I'll call you back. If you can, … if you need to detain them," he said, "lock them up, and we can send somebody out to look after the mother."

"That might be what has to happen," she said. "What I don't know is what kind of charges we're looking at, how severe the charges will be, whether the sisters will be eligible for community service to resolve this."

"And you know that's not for me to call," he said in a warning voice.

"I know that," she said quietly, "but I also know that a lot of the charges are up to you, depending on what we're actually looking at."

"Do you really think they're innocent in all of this?"

"No," she said, "absolutely not. Do I think that they did this out of greed or out of malice? No." She added, "Their initial misstep was to help their grandfather sign a property sales contract, when he wasn't of sound mind to do so. I do believe they were trying to fulfill his wishes, to care for the mother and the grandfather, but they should have gone through a legal process. They were also getting pressured to wrap up the sale by these same men, who were the ultimate buyers, and who went on to blackmail and to threaten them."

"Good God, what a nightmare," he said.

"I know," she said. "That's why I'm calling you. This one is above my pay grade."

He snorted at that. "We've always had pretty easy dealings around here up until now," he said. "I just didn't really expect something like this."

"Neither did I," she said. "So give me a hand and help me figure it out. Let me know when you can." With that, she hung up. She walked closer to the two women, with her fresh cup of coffee, and saw that Isabel had several pages written down, but Lana had barely started. "What's the matter, Lana?"

"Well, I just can't stop thinking about Mama."

"Yeah, and I just got off the phone with the prosecutor." Both women looked up hopefully. She shook her head. "He's looking into what the options are, but we can always get somebody from town to come collect your mother and get her settled into a care facility."

Both women cried out in horror.

Angela stared at them with a flat look and said, "Remember that part about not thinking about the consequences of your actions?"

"But you know Mama," Lana said. "You've had many a meal at our table."

"Yeah, and it breaks my heart to even think that her daughters would do this to her," she said, neatly turning the tables.

Both women flushed. They looked at each other and sagged in place.

"And I know we're not allowed to offer bribes or anything," Lana said, "but is there something we can do to make this better?"

"Yes, Lana," she said. "You two give us the information we need, and you cooperate fully. I can't guarantee that you will get off though. Walking into a jail and letting the prisoners out is hard to overlook. I can't guarantee that anybody'll give you a lenient sentence or will let you do time at home," she said, "but I can tell you that, if you don't cooperate, it'll be way worse."

The two women sat sniffling together and bent their heads to work on their statements.

Angela stared at these women she had known since they were all children. And it just shocked her. Lana was a little older and had always been a bit of an irresponsible flake, but apparently neither sister had really gotten on with a responsible life, and that just blew Angela away. She was reminded of the way Isabel had acted when Bonaparte had inquired about her identification, and she wondered what that was about. Although being forced to hand over her ID did make things seem more real, more official. And likely made Isabel realize what a mess she was in.

There were all kinds of lessons in life, but these two had each gone down a rabbit hole of sorts and apparently didn't see any way to get back out, making it worse instead of better. As Angela watched the two women weep over their statements, she felt like a heel, but too many things needed to be kept on course. She couldn't be a friend right now.

If it had been anybody else as the sheriff, Angela would have been here, with the sisters, advocating for them, but Angela couldn't do that now—and frankly wasn't so inclined. She was especially disappointed that Isabel hadn't told her that Lana was involved. That would have been a game-changer, so much so that Angela probably should have thought about it herself.

She pulled out her phone and checked for a text from Bonaparte, but there was nothing. She hated that even more. She knew it was too soon for him to have found, accosted, or even picked up one or the other of her escapees. And now that she actually needed four men to be picked up, she wondered if she should go grab Ronnie and former Deputy Johnson herself. She frowned at that idea, tossing it back and forth. If she locked the two women in the jail and put a padlock on it, that was possible. But if somebody came along and tried to cut that, she'd have nobody in the station to prevent it. And then she remembered her lack of a truck. She swore at that. Picking up the phone, she contacted the sheriff in the neighboring county. "Any chance you've got a deputy who can come over and sit in the jail to make sure nobody else gets out?"

"Yep," he said, "we can cover that. I'll have somebody there in about forty minutes."

"Good enough," she said. "I really appreciate it." And, with that, she hung up. The two women looked at her in surprise. "What?" she asked, with a raised eyebrow.

"You're getting help from another sheriff?" Isabel asked.

"Well, it depends on if the sheriff turns out to be on my side or not," she said bluntly. "Apparently all my deputies have run for the hills and quit."

At that, Lana flushed again. "He didn't want you to know."

"Maybe, but he didn't come to me either, did he? Just like you two should have just talked to me," she stated. "I've been the sheriff here for eight years. I've been your friend forever. I've lived here since birth."

They both winced. "I know," Lana said. "I told him that he should talk to you, but he didn't think you'd understand."

"Want to know what's hard for me to understand? It's deserting a sinking ship and leaving the captain here to handle everything," she said. "Johnson wanted a job, so I took him on and trained him, and I gave him that opportunity. Not only did he bail on me with the others but he allowed those keys to be used in a crime. You can bet I won't be doing that again."

"But that's all he wants, you know?" Lana said quietly.

"He just wants to come back to work."

"Yeah, and he should have thought about that before allowing his keys to be used to release prisoners from the jail," she said. "That won't get him invited back. Nor you for that matter." And, with that note of finality, she motioned at the statements and said, "Keep writing."

The two women frowned and looked at each other but bent their heads obediently and kept on writing out their statements.

Angela crossed her arms and waited. Then she grabbed a pad of paper and started writing down notes on the case herself. She had a big case report to write up, and things would get very confusing very quickly. So the sooner she got some of the facts straight in her own head, the better. And every time she thought she had it all down, something new would come up.

And every time something new would come up, she would check her phone to see if there was anything from Bonaparte. And there never was. Finally she groaned, tossed down her pen, pulled out her phone, and called him. When there was no answer, she started to panic. Then she took several long slow deep breaths. This was Bonaparte. This was one of Levi's men. She had to trust that he had this well in hand. If it were her deputies, that was a different story. But it wasn't. It was Bonaparte. She slowly replaced her phone, took a deep breath, picked up her pen, and continued on her report, hoping she had made the right decision.

BONAPARTE HAD ALREADY coasted past Johnny's place. The gate was locked. No vehicles were in the driveway, and all the lights were off. He kept on going down to Ronnie's place. Same thing. On a hunch, he headed back to Isabel's, where Henry and Johnny had been picked up from. As to why they would go back there, Bonaparte wasn't sure. Except maybe they expected Isabel to return.

As Bonaparte drove up, his instincts had him coming around to the back, where he parked. He also saw another vehicle there, parked off to the side. Thinking about that, he reversed and pulled around the corner again, so that anybody coming up to that vehicle wouldn't see his truck. As soon as he was parked, and the vehicle was locked up, he headed to Isabel's, going through the alley. Then he hit the public path and kept on walking toward the house.

As he approached, he stayed against the big trees along the back, while he studied the back wall. There hadn't been any vehicles in the front, and, outside of the one that he found parked in the alleyway, he wasn't sure who, if anyone, was here. It's quite possible that vehicle belonged to somebody else. He stayed in the shadows, silent and waiting, to see if any motion occurred.

When soft voices drifted through the windows, he smiled and bolted toward the kitchen, snugging up tight against the wall. Somebody was in there, and Isabel was still at the station. From underneath the window he listened to the conversation.

"We should just take out the bitch," stated a young punk, his voice whiny.

Henry.

An older, more granular voice snapped back in reply. "Once you start killing law enforcement," he said, "you'll bring everybody down on your back. It's one thing to kill any Joe Blow on the street, but take out a cop? Then you get every other branch of law enforcement looking for you, and you won't stay hidden for very long."

Johnny.

"But she's the one causing all the trouble. We got rid of all the deputies."

"No, we convinced the deputies to leave their posts, and, in several cases, no way they'll ever go back," the older man said, with a snigger. "That's the fun part, ruining lives."

"Yeah," Henry said, with enthusiasm. "I really like that part."

What he really meant was he liked being in control and having power, instead of being the one downtrodden and being picked on all the time.

Bonaparte understood, but it didn't make the punk an upstanding citizen. In this case, it made him a criminal.

Bonaparte moved silently toward the front of the house, hoping he would hear a third voice, but, so far, he heard just the two men. But that didn't mean Ronnie wasn't here. Seeing nobody on the front steps, Bonaparte hopped up, and without warning, stepped into the living room. The two men were sprawled on the couches. They looked up at him in shock and then, with a delayed reaction, bolted to their feet. He confirmed them as Johnny and Henry, from earlier in the day.

"Well, there we go," Bonaparte said, "the escapees. What do you know? Hands up." The fact that he had a handgun didn't register with the men. Johnny immediately reached for his gun on the coffee table, and Bonaparte winged him in the shoulder. He cried out, slammed against the couch, and stared at him in astonishment.

"Hey, you were going for a weapon against a law enforcement officer," Bonaparte said smoothly, his gaze hard and watchful. "If you think this wasn't a legal shooting, you're wrong."

But Henry swore at him. "You can't fucking shoot us," he said. "You're nobody. You're just another damn dumb deputy."

"Yep," he said, "I am. But I'm not one who scares easily. I'm not one who you'll run off. And you definitely won't ruin my life."

At that, he flushed. "What are you doing, listening in on our conversations now?"

"No, not at all," Bonaparte said. "It's much more a case of you guys shooting off your mouths." He walked over to where Johnny sat, his blood streaming over Isabel's couch. "Hands behind your back."

"I can't," he bit off. "I'm injured."

"Oh, come on. It's just a flesh wound," Bonaparte said, as he pulled handcuffs from his back pocket. Ignoring the shoulder wound, he disarmed him and snapped Johnny's hands together behind him, before shoving him back down on the couch. He turned to look at Henry, who was already sidling toward the front door.

"Go ahead, Henry," he said. "Head for that door, and I'll take you down before you hit the front gate."

Henry stopped and looked at him, then looked at the front door and bolted. Bonaparte didn't even waste time swearing and headed to the front door. He jumped all the porch steps in one huge leap and tackled Henry at the gate. Henry's head smacked down hard on the sidewalk, and he screamed for help. Bonaparte hopped to his feet, grabbed him, and stood him on his feet, then handcuffed him and said, "Now you're resisting arrest."

He walked him back up into the front of the house, parked him just inside the door, then walked over, grabbed

Johnny, and pulled the two of them out together, both swearing up a blue streak. Bonaparte ignored them and walked them around to the back of the house and over to his truck. He shoved them up into the back seat and slammed the door behind them.

"We can't even buckle our seat belts," Henry whined.

"I wouldn't worry about it," Bonaparte said. "That's really not on my radar."

"We'll get you for this," Johnny said, his voice low and ugly.

"Yeah? How's that working out for you so far?" he said. "You guys are nothing but punks. Punks with nothing behind you. You think money will fix everything for you."

"It will," Johnny said. "Money always does."

With their hands behind their backs like that, they were no danger to him. But he studied them carefully, as he backed out of the alley and headed toward the station. He put his phone on Speaker and called Angela.

She answered immediately. "Are you okay?"

"I'm fine," he said. "I'm bringing your two prisoners back."

"Now that is good news," she said. "What about Ronnie?"

"No sign of him yet."

"We also have to pick up Frank, my ex-deputy."

"Oh." Bonaparte thought about it and then nodded. "I gather he's the reason they got loose in the first place."

"Well, him and Lana, yes," she said.

"Okay, let's get these two back in first," he said. "Then I'll go round up Ronnie. Let me know where to find Frank."

As soon as Bonaparte hung up, Henry spoke up from behind him. "You'll never get him. You know that, right?"

"Why is that?" Bonaparte asked.

"Well, he's a deputy too, and you can't arrest a deputy."

"Well, he's not a deputy anymore," Bonaparte said, "and pretty soon he'll join you in jail."

Henry snorted at that. "That's not normal."

Bonaparte looked at the kid and shook his head. "You really are out of touch, aren't you?"

"I'm more in touch than you are, old man."

The *old man* comment stung a bit, but, considering Henry's age, it probably fit from his perspective. Then again, it didn't appear he had learned anything much so far or had been doing his learning in the wrong places. He certainly seemed to have a twisted view of how the law worked. But Bonaparte also noticed that Johnny didn't say anything. Punching in a speed dial number into his phone on the console of the truck, he called Angela. "Johnny will need medical attention when we get there."

"Did you shoot him?" she asked in a dry tone.

"Winged him in the top of the shoulder, as he was going for a weapon."

"Jesus," she said. "Too bad," she whispered.

"I hear you," he said.

"What about Henry?"

"He's got a bloody nose that he earned trying to escape."

"Of course he did," she said. "He's never been known to be all that bright."

With that, Bonaparte hung up, laughing.

Henry started swearing at him. "That's a lie," he said. "That's a damn lie. How dare she say that. She's nothing! Nothing but a piece of ass."

Bonaparte shook his head and said, "Wow, kid, you've really got some problems, don't you?"

When they finally pulled into the station, Angela came out and took possession of Henry, while Bonaparte escorted Johnny, and the four of them walked back into the jail cell. While there, she separated the two of them and brought in a nurse to look at Johnny's shoulder.

The nurse shrugged, then cleaned the wound. "It'll be fine," she said, then put a bandage on it and walked out. Johnny never said a word. She put Johnny back in with Henry in the same cell. In the other cell were the two sisters, sitting there, looking morose and lost.

Bonaparte stared at them and shook his head. "Wow," he said, "you two are a pair, aren't you?"

"We didn't have any choice," Lana said, glaring at him.

"You didn't have any choice but to let prisoners out of jail?"

She flushed at that. "I didn't think that one through," she said.

"You think?" he said. "Aiding and abetting criminals to escape? Does that ring a bell anywhere along the line? Have you heard any news media commentary on that? You know? How cops and sheriff's clerks go to jail for the same crimes as other people do?"

Lana just stared at him, all the color leaving her face. "I can't go to jail," she said. "I just can't. There's poor Mama to look after."

"And yet you didn't think about her before you walked in here and let criminals go free," he said in a dry tone. "Not to mention what they were doing to your sister when we arrested them."

"I can't go to jail." Lana hopped up and started shaking the bars. "Don't you hear me? I can't go to jail."

He stepped forward, shoved his face into hers, and,

without any sympathy, said, "News flash, you're already in jail."

And, with that, he turned and walked out.

Chapter 10

A NGELA REACHED UP and rubbed her forehead.

"You okay?" Bonaparte asked.

She nodded. "Yeah. My counterpart in a neighboring county is sending over a deputy to give me a hand."

"Good," he said. "Are you trying to get rid of me already?"

She shook her head. "No, but obviously we can't leave here, while that key is still missing."

"Right, that key," he said. "I can take care of that if you'll tell me where it's likely to be."

She handed him a piece of paper and said, "That's Frank's address."

He looked at it, nodded, and said, "I can almost walk from here."

"It wouldn't be a bad idea to walk him back over in handcuffs either," she said sadly. "It's too bad. He was a very promising deputy."

"Well, looks like they got to him one way or another."

"And Lana now says he doesn't know she took the keys."

"Do you believe her?"

"Nope," she said, "I don't. Earlier she said he was trying to get copies made. I expect the brothers have something on him too. Whether it was big or not, I don't know, but he didn't come to me with it."

"No," he said, "they never seem to, do they?"

"Apparently I'm not anywhere near as approachable as I thought I was, and that is something I'll just have to live with."

"It takes something like this to figure out what the culture is around you," he said. "Don't take it personally."

She looked up at him in surprise. "How the hell else can I take it?" she cried out. "Look at this place? I mean, it's like rats deserting a ship."

"It's more like rats finding their own level because a bigger rat came into town. They figured that rat would take over, so, instead of standing with you to fight him, they were gutless and bet against you, siding with him."

"Right. Eight years," she said. "Eight years I've been here in this position."

"And you've done a good job," he said. "You've got very little crime, and everybody has been happy, until the two guys with money moved in. And, by the way, Levi found out there is a move for a major highway to go through here."

She stared at him in shock. "What? A highway? We haven't heard anything about it. There's been no public meetings or announcements. Not even rumors."

"No, it's being pushed through at the state level," he said. "And, yes, it looks like your property is likely to be affected."

She stood up slowly. "What?"

He nodded. "Which also affects the other properties that you've been talking about, which is why the brothers were trying to buy up everything. Because, once that highway goes through, a ton of commercialism is about to happen here, and they want in on the action."

She just stared at him, her stomach twisting. "And what

about my place?"

"Well, that's part of the question, isn't it?" he said. "Obviously you didn't know anything about this."

"Nope, I didn't," she said, reaching for the phone.

"Who are you calling?"

"A council member," she said. "Let's see what he has to say for himself."

"Chances are good he may not even know very much about this."

"Well, if he doesn't, it's high time he does," she said shortly. "Because somebody needs to put a stop to this."

"You know it won't be that easy."

"No," she said, "it won't be. But it doesn't have to be that hard either. Who the hell is driving this? This is literally the first I've heard of it," she said, sitting back down and staring at him in shock.

"Which is why I'm telling you, and Levi told me, so he knows more about it than I do."

She nodded and said, "You know what? That's a good point. I'll call Levi first." She disconnected her call.

He smiled. "Good idea. If anybody can give you a hand with this, it's him."

She immediately dialed and connected with Ice. As soon as Angela identified herself, Ice's warm tone broke over her, like the soothing hug of a friend.

"Hey, sweetie. Sounds like you got yourself a spot of trouble up there."

"I sure do," she said. "Thanks so much for sending Bonaparte. He's been a huge help already."

"Nothing like finding out nobody's got your back," Ice said quietly. "Just remember. We always have yours."

"That's actually another reason I'm calling," she said.

"I'm wondering if I could ask a favor."

"Anything," Ice said. "Ask away."

Then she brought up what Levi had told Bonaparte. "He mentioned that to me," Ice said thoughtfully. "I don't think they can push stuff like that through, but it seems like somebody is trying. Let me think on this for a bit."

Almost immediately after hanging up from Ice's call and after getting everybody set up into their jail cells, her new borrowed deputy arrived. With relief, she asked him to watch the cells and warned him about what had happened earlier.

He nodded. "That's fine. I don't know any of the people in this town," he said, checking out the four in the cells, "but, looking at this bunch, apparently I don't want to either."

They all just glared back at him.

He shrugged and locked the doors to the basement itself. "I've got this. Go pick up your next prisoner."

Angela and Bonaparte smiled and headed out. As they walked outside, Bonaparte looked at her and said, "This has been one hell of a weekend."

She nodded. "Yeah, especially if we can pick up Ronnie." They both climbed in Bonaparte's truck.

"What will you do to keep them here?"

"That'll be the trouble."

"And what about their lawyers?"

"Not my problem," she said. "The prisoners are here in jail now and hopefully they'll stay there until Monday morning, when the circuit judge comes."

"That should be fun."

"Not so much. The prosecutor is working on it as well. I did update him by a text that we had our prisoners back and that we're headed to pick up another couple."

"I'm sure he loved that too."

"Everybody loves to get called about work on weekends," she said, with a smile.

"I don't have a problem with it," he said. "At least I know that I'm doing what I need to do."

"Exactly," she said. "I get that a Monday-through-Friday eight-to-four schedule works for a lot of jobs, but it doesn't necessarily work for law enforcement. It seems like the criminals have more time for crossing that line on the weekends than any other time."

"How does that work?" he said. "You'd think they'd want a day off too."

She burst out laughing. "A lot of times these guys are working Monday to Friday at some low-level day job but also spend their weekends either getting into trouble or trying to make more money on the side. It's just that they haven't found a way or don't have the patience to do it legally."

"You're right about the lack of the patience. I think it's too slow of a process when it's legal," he said. "Everybody wants a shortcut."

"Isn't that the truth?" she said, with a shake of her head. "I never really found that to work so well for me."

"Me either," he said.

She grinned. "But you love working for Levi, don't you?"

"Yeah, I really do. I like all the guys and the whole camaraderie of a larger pool of people you know you can count on."

"Do they usually send you guys out alone?"

"Sometimes," he said, with a shrug. "It depends on what

the job is."

"So this was just a small job then," she teased. "I mean, he only sent you, after all."

"Or it's a big job," he said, with a cheeky grin, "and he needed a big guy."

She burst out laughing again, absolutely loving the camaraderie of being around him.

"It's nice to see somebody with a smiling face," he commented.

She looked at him in surprise. "Don't you see very many smiling faces?"

"Not when this kind of stuff comes down."

"Well, that's because everybody is worried," she said.

"Those two women back there," he said, "have you thought about what's happening to their mama and grandfather?"

"Well, hopefully we'll stop by and take a look at that today. If not, there's already a call out for Mama to get picked up and taken to a home."

"That would be hard on her," he said.

"It may be," she said. "But again, the authorities need to deal with that issue without me. And depending on how their mother's doing with her treatments and all, she may do fine on her own."

"Or she could be completely dependent and need a caregiver," he said quietly.

She sighed. "I know, and I don't know what I'm supposed to do about it."

"Nothing you can do."

"It depends on the prosecutor at this point," she said, with a shrug. "It would be nice if they could work something out."

"Maybe at least the sisters could get out on bail, … if they can post bail."

"I think they probably can," she said, with a frown, "though I've been surprised by those two. So I'm not betting on anything at this point." She sent the prosecutor another text message about the two of them, reminding him that they had a deadline for help with their mama's care. She shook her head at the whole mess. "It would sure be nice if we could pick up Ronnie now then go home and have a barbecue."

"Hell yeah," he said. "I'm pretty sure you owe me that."

"Owe you what?" she asked in astonishment.

"Hey, you promised me barbecued ribs."

"No, *you* promised *me* barbecued ribs," she said, with a laugh.

He shrugged. "Same diff."

She shook her head. "Not in anybody's dreams is that the same diff," she snickered. They went to Frank's house first, only no one was there. Frowning she said, "We'll try Ronnie first then come back to Frank's later."

They drove up to Ronnie's place. She looked at the gate and said, "It's locked of course."

"Yep, and do you think it was him shooting at the house earlier?"

"I don't know," she said. "I mean, it should have been Ronnie, since his house is closest to mine, and that's where we saw him go, but it didn't really look that much like him."

"Who did it look like?"

"Neither of the brothers honestly," she said, with a shrug. "You've seen Johnny, and he's a pretty average height, average build, but Ronnie is taller, as you saw at the restaurant."

"Okay, well let's go see what he's got to say for himself." They pulled up to the gate, and Bonaparte hit the button to be let through. But, of course, nobody answered. She hopped out, walked around, and hit it again, identifying herself. Again there was no answer. He looked at her and said, "What's his incentive to actually answer?"

"None I can think of," she said, "but we don't have any rights to go on the property either."

"*Hmm*, I thought he was involved in this coercion deal. Doesn't that give us the right to pick him up?"

"Yes, but I'll have to get a warrant to force our way onto the property, if he'll play hard to get." She called the prosecutor and explained the problem.

"Do you even know that he's home?" he asked.

"No. I can't confirm it at this time."

"Can you get confirmation for me?"

"We can just go find out for ourselves."

"You could," he said. "I'll call you back."

Pocketing the phone, she looked at Bonaparte and said, "He'll call me back."

He just rolled his eyes.

"I know," she said, "bureaucracy at its best."

"Or its worst. We need access. We need to know if Ronnie's in there, and we need to know now," he said.

She thought about it, nodded. "I know. We came here to pick him up, but we have to make sure that everything is locked up and as legal as we can make it, so it doesn't get thrown out in court." Just then she got a phone call. It was the prosecutor.

"Fine," he said. "I've got a judge on standby, and we're working on the warrant right now. Call you back."

She smiled and gave Bonaparte a thumbs-up. "They're

working on it."

"Good," he said, "because it looks like we're about to get company."

She looked down the driveway, and a sports car came toward them. "Wow," she said, "this could be fun."

"Only if it's him," he said.

But, as Angela watched, a young woman was driving.

She came to the gate, opened it, and looked at them. "I can't even get out with you parked like that," she said, glaring at Bonaparte. "Really, like if some people would just learn to drive, you know?"

"Who are you?" Angela asked.

The woman tilted her head. "I'm Maisie," she said. "Why? And who are you anyway?"

"I'm the sheriff," she said. "Is Ronnie in there?"

"Yeah, and he's in a hell of a mood too," she said. "I'm leaving, until he's not so grumpy."

"That's probably wise," she said. "We need to talk to him."

"Go on in," she said. "I don't have a problem with you talking to him. Who knows? Maybe you'll get him in a better mood!"

At that, Bonaparte backed up a bit, so she could get by his truck, and Angela hopped up into the front seat and said, "Let's go." He drove through the gate as soon as Maisie went through, before the gate could close.

Looking at Angela, he said, "Convenient of her to invite us in."

"I'm not sure how convenient it'll be for him, but Maisie definitely invited us in." And Angela gave him a wolfish smile. "Besides, the warrant just came through as well." He looked at her in surprise, as she nodded. "Coercion and blackmail don't go over well here."

"So we subdue our prisoner and then get a free-for-all at his place."

"Well, hardly a free-for-all," she said. "I haven't got the warrant in hand, so I don't know exactly what it covers."

"Well, it sure as hell better cover his electronics and all the rest of that shit."

"I would hope so too," she said, "but I have to wait for that to come in."

"Well, to do all that, yes, we do," he said, "but not for picking him up, right?"

"No," she said, "not for that."

At the doorway, they knocked, and, at the first clip of knuckles against wood, the door opened, and Ronnie stood there, glaring at them.

"You're trespassing," he said, holding up his phone. "I already have my lawyer ready to dial," he said, sneering and speaking directly to Angela. "Obviously I can't call law enforcement, when it's so corrupt."

"Interesting," she said. "You see? We have full rights to be here. For one thing, we were actually welcomed onto the property." She caught the surprise in his eyes, as he looked down the driveway, and then a frown appeared.

She nodded. "Your lovely girlfriend Maisie told us to come on up," she said. "So here we are." Smiling, she went on. "However, we do have a warrant, and we're actually here to take you in for questioning." He looked at her and moved back several steps.

"Like hell you are," he said, his fingers pressing Call on the phone.

"Oh, I think it's more than that," she said, looking over at Bonaparte. "Do you want the honors?"

Bonaparte smiled and stepped forward, and she knew that anybody with half a brain would have felt some fear or at least respected his obvious physical superiority and complied, but these guys were not very smart. Ronnie was also starting to look a little on the seedy side.

"I'm not going anywhere with you," Ronnie said. "You lay your hand on me," he said, "and I'll have you arrested."

"You can try, but, if you're resisting arrest, it'll just get much harder."

Ronnie shook his head. "You've got nothing on me. I didn't do anything."

"That's not quite what Johnny and Henry are saying," she said. "Or the two women."

He looked at Angela in surprise. "What? You mean, *your* friends?"

"Hardly," she said cheerfully. "Not when they're criminals and when they've put themselves on separate sides of a legal issue. But now that's not up to me. That's for the prosecutors to resolve. And I don't really care how you feel about this. If you won't come calmly and quietly, you'll be resisting arrest, so do your worst."

He backed up several steps, his hands up to ward off Bonaparte's approach. "He'll just beat me up."

"He's never beaten up anybody who didn't need it," she said quite cheerfully. Her phone buzzed just then, and she nodded in satisfaction and said, "Oh, good, we have the warrant in hand now."

"I want to read it," Ronnie shouted.

"Well, you could," she said, "if you went to the station. But, at the moment, we're more concerned about securing our prisoner," she said, with a hard look at him.

"What are the charges?"

"Well, I don't have the complete list at hand right now," she said, "but we'll start with embezzling, kidnapping, coercion, threats, and any number of other things. We might even get ourselves worked up to murder."

At that, he stopped and stared.

She nodded quietly. "In case you haven't figured it out," she said, "the game is up."

"It's not up," he said in a mean, vindictive voice. "It's only just started."

"Says you," she said in a bored tone, and, at that, Bonaparte moved so damn fast that Ronnie didn't have a chance to do anything.

"Pretty damn sure if we check that vehicle hidden in the tree line, we can probably match it to the Hummer from my dash cam that tried to run us off the road too," Bonaparte said. "Was that an employee of yours? Or just a friend?"

The guy looked at him. "What's the matter? You don't even know how to drive?"

"Depends," Angela said, "if driving also means trying to run people off the road. I mean, we'll have to see about an attempted murder charge there—of a sheriff and her deputy." She watched as Bonaparte quickly handcuffed Ronnie and sat him down in a chair. She asked Bonaparte, "Do you want to run him back to the jail?"

"Really could use a few more deputies," he said, looking at her.

She nodded. "I know, but I need him back in the jail and separated from the others."

"Fine," he said. "But I don't really like the idea of you staying here alone."

She grinned at him. "Glad to know you care," she said cheerfully. "But, on the other hand, I am the sheriff," and, with that, was a very quiet reminder of who was the boss.

He looked at her sideways, gave a clipped nod, and said, "Point to you." He walked over and stood Ronnie back up on his feet, then together they led Ronnie out to the truck and loaded him in the back. "I'll take him down and be right back."

"You do that," she said, then stood there with her hands on her hips, waiting for them to disappear, before heading back inside. She pulled up the warrant on her phone and quickly read through it. When she found it included all electronics, she whooped and turned around to get started, only to find herself facing a handgun pointed right at her. She didn't recognize his face or know his name, but the shape of his body matched the man who shot into her house. And she could never mistake the look on his face, filled with sheer and utter hatred. She looked at him. "Are you going to pull that trigger?"

"Hell, yes, I'll pull that trigger," he said, "and there's not a damn person in the world who can stop me."

Without even thinking, she quickly raised her right leg hard and kicked his gun arm, the gun firing into the ceiling, then she followed it up with a hard right, a move her father had taught her a long time ago. While his head snapped back, her leg shot out to hook his legs and to pull them out from under him. He slammed down hard, flat on his back on the hardwood floor, and lay still. She pulled out her phone, called Bonaparte, and said, "Better get back here."

She checked the man over, but he was unconscious. She could already hear the truck racing up the driveway to the front door. Even though it had been just a few minutes, he probably hadn't even made it out of the gate yet. Bonaparte ran into the house, stopped when he saw the guy on the ground and the handgun on the floor beside him. "Shit," he said.

"Yeah," she replied. "We didn't check the building first. That's my fault."

"This is the guy who shot into the house?"

"Looks like it to me. He's the one carrying the rifle, that you picked up."

"Well, damn," he said. "Who the hell is he?"

"Don't know yet," she said, then reached down and pulled a wallet from the prone man's pocket. "Looks like it's either a brother or a cousin," she said. "Same last name." She held it out for him.

"Might be an uncle or older brother or something, based on his age," he said.

"That's quite possible," she said, looking down at him, and sighed. "We'll have to get his head checked out."

"Maybe I'll bring our prisoner in and see if he can ID him."

"Or maybe just mention that you've got to call for an ambulance for an old man who attacked the sheriff, and maybe Ronnie'll start talking all over himself."

Bonaparte looked at her and nodded. "You know what? I think that's a damn good idea. Time to go poke the rattler." With that, he turned to head back outside.

She wanted to join him, but, at the same time, no way would she leave this guy injured and on the floor. Just too many chances of another rattler coming back to life.

Bonaparte pulled up short and turned around, while she stood here. He took one look, shook his head, and said, "You keep him here, and I'll go check out the rest of the house, before I head outside." She nodded and waited while he did a full search, then came back and asked, "Did you call somebody for him?"

She nodded. "Yeah, I've got an ambulance coming."

"But you have nobody to stand watch at the hospital," he said.

She shook her head. "No, I don't. Man, it sucks being shorthanded."

"That it does."

The ambulance came in not very long afterward. And once they had the prisoner collected, she warned them that he was her prisoner and needed to be kept at the hospital under guard. She handcuffed him to the gurney railing. She said, "I'll get a guard and have him there as soon as you're at the hospital."

Once they left, Bonaparte turned to her and said, "Who have you got to use for a guard?"

She said, "I'll have to hire somebody private." She pulled out her phone and called someone she'd used in the past.

When Jerry answered, his tone was genial and bright. "Hey, Sheriff. Have you got work for me?"

"I do, if you're looking for some and if I can trust you."

Immediately there was silence on the other end. "Wow, I've never had that asked of me before," he said.

"Things are a little different these days," she said grimly. "We're under a bit of a siege right now."

"Oh, I know," he said. "I was hoping you might bring me in to help out, but you didn't."

"Partly because I already have somebody else, but we're really short-staffed, so I need you too."

"Right. So," he said, "what do you want me to do?" She quickly explained the situation, and he said, "I'll be at the hospital in a few minutes. I'm already getting changed."

"He doesn't leave at all. Got it?"

"Got it," he said.

"And nobody takes him away. Not lawyers or anybody else," she said.

"Got it, Sheriff," he said. "He won't get away."

"Good," she said, "because somebody turned my prisoners out of the jail cell once already today, so I'm not taking any chances."

After a moment of silence on the other end, he exploded. "What?"

"You heard me," she said, "so I'm counting on you to make sure this guy doesn't leave."

"I got this," he said. "And I'm looking for full-time work, by the way. Anytime you need me, I can drop my part-time gigs and be there. And, Sheriff, you can trust me."

"I'll keep it in mind, Jerry. Thank you." After she was off the phone, Bonaparte looked at her, and she nodded. "He's decent. I was thinking about bringing him on as a deputy before. And then this all blew up and …"

"And you didn't know who you could trust anymore."

"Exactly, and I didn't want to put anybody in a position they weren't comfortable with," she added.

"Well, that's fine and dandy," he said, "but not good when we've got this situation."

"I know, and I almost asked Levi for more help."

"Not a bad idea," he said. "We can always call him and get more help coming."

"We'll see what it's like after this," she said. "I really hate to impact him any more than I have to. He's already been very generous with supplying you."

"Well, I'm hardly a parts department, and neither is Levi," he said. "We come because people need us."

"And it's appreciated very much," she said, then looked

at him. "Can you take the prisoner to the jail now?"

"Yep, I got it," he said. "now that I've searched the place, you should be fine. Also there's no dog in residence today."

"Okay but remember, it's not for you to look after me," she said gently.

He stood straight, bringing himself up to his full height, and said, "Well, whether it is or not isn't the issue," he said. "I will never ever let somebody handle something alone if it's obvious they need help." And, with that, he turned and walked out.

BONAPARTE THOUGHT ABOUT her words as he drove to the station. She obviously had been alone for a little too long. Or maybe she had deputies that she hadn't felt she could actually count on. If they were young kids, that would explain it too, especially if they were still trying to figure out what was right and wrong within their own manhood. Bonaparte had no doubts how to handle life. But, if he'd been nineteen or twenty, or even a little older, that could be a different story. He pulled into the station not long afterward, opened up the back door to his truck, and helped out his prisoner. The glaring man didn't say a word, as Bonaparte walked Ronnie inside the station and down to the jail.

As soon as he got there, the other deputy hopped up, looked at him in surprise, and said, "Another one, huh?"

Bonaparte nodded and said, "Yeah, and one more headed to the hospital. We still need to pick up Frank as well."

"Jesus," he said, "you guys are picking them up all over the place."

"Well, you keep hold of this one. Let's put him opposite his buddy. They quickly unlocked the cell and moved him in with Johnny. Bonaparte removed the handcuffs and then locked the cell back up. "Make sure nobody comes in or out," he warned.

"Got it," the deputy said. He looked at the five of them and shook his head. "Unless you're expecting somebody to break them out."

"I wouldn't be at all surprised," he said, "but hopefully not in the next ten minutes."

At that, the deputy rolled his eyes. "I might just call in some friends," he said.

"If you feel you need some backup, then let me know now," he said, "because we can't afford to have these guys walk again."

"They're not walking," he said. "I've got some buddies not too far away, in case I need help."

"Yeah, but which side of this war are they on?"

He looked at him in surprise and said, "You know what? That's a damn fine question. I'll find out. If you come back, and they're sitting here, drinking coffee with me, then you'll know they're on our side."

"Just make sure that you don't just *think* they're on your side, but, when we walk in, we're the ones who get attacked."

He winced at that. "Well, I wouldn't have believed that, but you're right. Let me think about that." He asked, "Where are you heading next?"

"Back to support the sheriff. She's got a warrant on these guys in the one house for now."

"What do we expect to find?"

"Quite possibly proof of murder."

He stared at him in shock. "Wow, who knew this town was so full of trouble."

"Yeah, it's a hell of a mess," he said. "You been around

here long?"

"Nope, not very long at all. She's a good sheriff. I know most of the guys in my station hold her in high respect. My sheriff definitely does. I thought the townsfolk here did too," he said.

"Well, something rotten has been going on here for a little while," Bonaparte said, "but I don't know if it's really the town or if it's all tied up with these guys here," he said, with a head tilt toward the jail cell behind him.

"You're probably right there."

"But still, there's got to be a reason for the weakness in the first place."

"Just people," the deputy said gently. "Just people."

Bonaparte thought about that, as he raced back toward the property where Angela was. He hated to leave her alone, but he had to honor the fact that she was a sheriff in her own right and fully capable of handling most of these situations. He had worked with many female law enforcement officers over the years, but, for whatever reason, this one was getting to him. Not in a bad way, in a good way. Maybe too good. He really liked who she was. And he was always a big champion of the underdog.

But, of course, Levi's words still rang in his head, as he thought about the matchmaking angle. In a way Bonaparte with Angela was a good match. She was definitely Bonaparte's kind of person. She was also tall, slim, fit, and sexy as hell. She had that little dimple in her left cheek that he couldn't stop staring at. She held herself with strong shoulders and a straight back and stared at the world calmly but head-on. He had to admire that.

Even when she was under the gun, like she was now, she wasn't folding. She stood up for the cause and for the job she'd taken on. Again, something he couldn't do anything but respect. Then he realized he was trying to find faults in order to not fall head over heels. It had been a long time since he'd had a relationship, ... at least one that he wanted long-term. But that seemed to be where he was heading right now, which was just the weirdest thing. Still, he pulled up to the gate, happy to see it remained wide open. Parking in front of the house, he took three big steps inside and called out for her.

"Angela? Where are you?"

He heard her faint voice responding upstairs. He raced up and found her standing in the middle of the master bedroom. "Have you found anything?"

"No," she said. "Nothing in the office downstairs. No electronics, no laptops, no nothing." He grimaced. She nodded. "I know, right? It's got to be here somewhere. I just don't know where."

"And you've checked the night tables and all the usual places in here?"

"I have," she said, "and there's nothing, but now I'm intrigued by this wall."

He studied the wall, wondering what she was getting at.

"It feels like it's short."

"What do you mean by short?" he asked.

"I've been through the rest of the house, and it just seems like that wall is off," she said, pointing to the wall she faced, "like it should have been pushed out another six feet."

He walked closer, studied it, and nodded, as he ran his hands over the paneling. "I wouldn't be at all surprised if a panic room was on the other side."

"Considering the money they put into this place, I could see that as well," she said, "although I wouldn't necessarily have put it in the master bedroom."

"I would," he said. "A lot of guys retreat to their bedrooms when it comes to this kind of stuff, so, in a way, it makes total sense." He kept at it, carefully running his hands over the surface of the wall, and it didn't take him long before his fingers felt a faint ridge. He hooked his fingernail into it and followed it up to the top. He looked at her, and she nodded, then stepped forward.

"Look. The pattern is off here too." She reached out a palm and pressed gently. Almost instantly the section snapped closed and pushed in, then popped out.

He pulled it open and whistled. "Now this is more like it." The two of them stepped into what looked like a very intense high-security room. Not only were security cameras all around but also laptops and workstations.

"Do you think it's just for him in here?" she asked, "I'm puzzled because it's way bigger than the six feet I thought it would be."

"Well, this room certainly could handle more than one person, so it's probably mostly for him and his buddies."

"That would make sense too. Maybe this is the only room like this. Or do you think we have another one at Johnny's place?"

"You know what? I suspect this will be the control center. And maybe a backup hidden room is at Johnny's house."

"Good to note," she said. "If we can just get through this stuff here, it'll be huge for my case."

"The only thing," he said, "and please don't take this wrong. But do you want to bring in Denver for this?"

"I've already thought of that," she said, "and I spoke to one of the council members earlier. He told me that some of them know about a file that Denver has already opened up on this crew."

Bonaparte nodded. "Which means that you can do what you want, but chances are Denver will take it over anyway."

"It's still my jurisdiction, my case," she said, glaring at him.

He held up his hands. "I know, and I'm happy to take all this back to the station and go through it myself. And, if we need any more hackers," he said, "you know Levi's got you covered there."

She nodded slowly. "I think the first thing is to confiscate all of this and take it in for evidence."

"Yet you don't have anybody to do that for you, do you?"

She looked at him, shook her head. "Nope."

"And what about forensics?" he said, "Do you have anybody?"

"No," she said. "I have to go to Denver for that."

"So why don't you start there now?"

She nodded. "I guess that probably a good idea." And from there, it was organized chaos, at least as organized as they could make it. They went systematically through all the equipment, dismantling everything so they could take it back to the office and reconstruct it all there.

"It seems like a waste," he murmured.

"I can't deal with it all here," she said, staring around the security room. "We've taken photos of everything, and now we have all the equipment ready to transport."

"What happens when Ronnie finds out what you've taken?"

"He'll set his lawyers on me, which is why I wanted to get it out of here."

Just then her phone rang. "It's Denver." She spoke with

someone from forensics there. "Yes, we're removing everything and bringing it back to the station." At that, another voice interrupted, and she realized they really would take this over. She frowned into the phone. "I don't want to hand all this off to your case, when it's also my case," she said heatedly, turning to look at Bonaparte, putting her phone on Speaker.

"We're taking it over," the man said.

"I'm not sure you have any jurisdiction to do that," she said in a defiant voice. There was silence on the other end.

"It will be a joint task force, of course."

"Right. Of course it will be," she said in a dry tone. At that, she watched as Bonaparte set one laptop back down again, opened it up, and pulled out a chair. She said, "We'll be hours yet."

"And you don't have the facilities there to handle this. This isn't just about Denver," he said. "This could go across the country."

She winced at that. "In which case, you're bringing in the FBI? Is that what I'm hearing?"

"It's not typically one of their cases," the man cautioned.

"Maybe not, but, if you expect me to be cooperative to the extent that you're taking this over," she said, "I want to make sure that you aren't as corrupt as the people who started this."

An audible gasp could be heard at the other end, and she looked up to see Bonaparte staring at her, his eyebrows raised.

She said, "No offense intended, but it's obvious that some level of collusion has occurred, which involves some top officials in Denver," she said. "And it's my duty to ensure you aren't a part of it."

"That's a pretty broad accusation," he said.

"I get it, but it's one that needs to be brought up."

"I'll give you that," he said, "but I don't know just how I'm supposed to convince you that I'm innocent."

"Well, I'll make a few inquiries on my own, and then I'll call you back," she snapped. She hung up the phone and stood there, glaring at Bonaparte. He smiled, then clapped gently. She shrugged. "It's obvious these brothers are getting some assistance from somebody in Denver," she said.

"And much higher perhaps," he said.

"I know." She pulled out her phone and, as soon as Levi answered, she explained what had just happened.

"Give me a little time, and I'll get back to you," he said, and he hung up.

Chapter 11

A NGELA LOOKED OVER at Bonaparte. "What would we do without guys like Levi?"

"Wander around in the dark," he said quietly. "We need people doing what he does. It's really necessary and nice to have somebody who's unbiased helping out. Plus he and Ice have some of the best people, who are all fast and expert at what they do."

She nodded, waiting for Levi to call, then noted Bonaparte doing something on the laptop. "What are you doing?" she asked.

"Checking to see just what information is here," he said.

"A whole server is here," she murmured, looking over his shoulder.

He nodded. "But we don't want Denver or even the FBI to have everything without a backup."

She frowned at that. "What should we do then?"

"Well, I have a thumb drive on my key chain," he said. "It's a USB, so we can transfer a bunch of information, if need be. I'm just studying this to make sure we actually have something solid."

"Now I feel useless," she said, looking around.

"There's another laptop," he said and pointed to the one he had put on a stack.

She immediately popped it open, turned it on, and said,

"The email program is open."

"Good," he said. "You might want to start taking some photos. Get his various email addresses that we can then search through for anything we might need, plus hopefully some log-ins."

She laughed. "Ronnie, the idiot, has a file called Passwords."

Bonaparte looked up. "Really?"

Nodding, she opened it up and started taking photos.

"What we really need to know is what's going on with this property development angle," he said. "And anything they may have done in the meantime."

While working on that, she shifted the laptop, since the stack it rested on was a little precarious. She pulled a notebook out from underneath it, and, flipping through it, realized it was mostly empty. Then she turned it around because it was one of those that had a front cover on either side. She stopped, checking out both covers, front and back, then went through the first few pages from each side. She was stunned to see the information and note-taking written there.

Remove deputies.
Sheriff cooperates or take her out.

As she mumbled the words, he looked up, distracted. "What are you reading?" he asked. She held out the notebook. "Looks like somebody's doodles," he said, studying the page. "But not doodles we particularly like to see."

"Yeah, especially not the part about taking out the sheriff," she said, shaking her head.

"No, but that's not a shock either," he said. "It's nothing more than we've already seen signs of, right?"

"I know," she said. Her phone rang at that moment. She looked at it, smiled, and said, "Hey, Levi. What's up?"

"I'm sending two men from Denver your way."

"Okay," she said, "but why?"

"Because I trust them," he said.

"Well, I'm happy to hear that," she said. "I presume that means you're not trusting anybody else?"

"I pulled the governor's ear," Levi said. "We have to get to the bottom of this, and we can't trust anybody at the moment."

"Good enough," she said. "So how will I know who they are?"

"Do you remember Stone?"

"Are you kidding? How could I not remember Stone?" she said, laughing. "He's very memorable."

"He is, indeed. And he happens to be in Denver."

"Oh, yay," she said, turning to look at Bonaparte, who now straightened up and stared at her in surprise. "Is he coming with them?"

"He is, and he's also one of our best hackers."

"Yes, I've heard about his skills," she said. "I'm actually quite delighted. How far out are they?"

"With any luck the good guys will be there in ten minutes."

"Is that before or after the forensic team from Denver gets here?"

"I'm not sure, but Stone and his men take priority," he said. "You hand off nothing until he gets there."

"Well, if there'll be a fight," she said, "I need some legal leg to stand on."

"Stone has it with him. It's coming directly from the governor."

"Good enough," she said, then hung up the phone. She looked at Bonaparte. "Well, this will be interesting."

"Hey, we couldn't ask for a better person in our back pocket than Stone. Both for hacking and for a scuffle."

"Oh, I agree," she said. "It'll just be a matter of who gets here first."

"Doesn't matter who gets here first," he said. "Nothing leaves without Stone."

She looked at the laptop in his hands. "Did you find anything?"

"All kinds of shit," he said. "Ronnie's got folders in here, with access to a lot of details on business dealings."

"Well, if we do end up in trouble," she said, "and have to hand everything over, I suggest we keep that one back, out of everybody's possession, unless you can get it all saved to that thumb drive before those Denver people arrive."

He looked at it, with a slow dawning smile. "I like the way you think."

"I just want to make sure," she said, "that the brothers don't get away scot-free."

"Nope, that's not happening." Just then they heard a vehicle.

She looked over at him, sighed, and said, "What do you want to bet we'll have an entirely different fight on our hands right now?"

He immediately closed the lid and placed the laptop on the bed, and said, "Come on." She headed downstairs with him at her side.

When they got to the front door, she stepped out and froze.

BONAPARTE JOINED ANGELA and took a look at the two forensic vans, clearly marked Denver County, Colorado, that had just pulled up with a team of six. Bonaparte looked at them, crossed his arms over his chest, and said, "Where's your authorization?"

The team looked at him in surprise, then at her. "Sheriff Angela Zimmerman?"

She nodded. "Yes, that's correct, but we're waiting on three other men right now," she said. "So I can't give you access yet."

"We came here under Commander Conrad's instructions," the head tech said, frowning at her.

"And I get that, but I still can't give you access." She gave him a cheery smile.

"Surely this isn't a jurisdictional issue," he said, his hands on his hips. "You don't have the equipment or facilities to even begin to handle something like this."

"You're right," she said, with a gentle nod. "Absolutely correct. And most of this stuff should go to Denver theoretically. The trouble is, I don't know who I can trust at this point." At that, she could see the shock rippling through the team, as they looked at each other, then looked at her. "You see? Some of this information leads right back to Denver and beyond," she said. "So we have to make sure that this material stays in the right hands."

"Well, that would be us. That was the whole point of us coming out here personally," he said, crossing his arms and leaning against one of the vehicles.

"Yes, and maybe no," she said, looking over at Bonaparte. "You want to keep him here for a few minutes." He nodded, and she walked back inside. He didn't know what she was doing but assumed she was probably checking to see where the hell Stone was. When the men started toward him, he held up a hand and said, "*Uh-uh-uh.*"

"Look. We came here to do this job," he said. "If you want, we can call in our own bosses."

"Oh, absolutely," he said, "please do." One of the men stepped off to the side, pulled out his phone, and made a call.

Bonaparte just waited because, of course, there would be a lot of official red tape and people who were really pissed off to get through to finally get anywhere.

"I don't get it," one of the other techs said. "Didn't you call us?"

"Well, not necessarily," Bonaparte said. "Somebody did. We just have to figure out who's pulling the strings here." As he watched the horizon, a cloud of dust rose, heading their way. He relaxed slightly, thinking it was Stone. But, as it got closer, he looked grim. No way that black smoky vehicle would be his guys. At least he didn't think so, although it did have a government look to it. As it pulled up, a stranger hopped out.

"What's going on?" asked the guy in the suit, eyeing six forensic techs standing idly on the front lawn.

"You know what's going on," Bonaparte said. "You're not taking anything from this house."

"No, that's not quite true. I don't know who you are," he said, with a wave of his hand. "You may well be some big muscle-bound idiot," he said, "but, in the end, you're just a deputy. You have no authority here."

At that, Angela stepped out from inside the living room. "No need to insult my deputy," she said. "I'm the sheriff here, and this is my jurisdiction. Shall we discuss just what it is you're trying to pull right now by showing up here?"

"You know exactly what I'm trying to pull," he sneered.

She shook her head. "I really wouldn't go there if I were you. You see? I'm looking to identify just who is crooked in Denver and participating in this scheme."

At that, the techs stopped, looked at each other, and visibly stepped back, as if not wanting to get in the crosshairs.

The man glared at her. "You're stepping into very big boots right now."

"My boots are plenty big," she said. "I've been on the job for a long time, and I've seen an awful lot of politicians come and go."

He stood there, his hands on his hips, and said, "I can order you to stand down."

"Well, you could," she said, "except you're not my boss."

"You're out of your jurisdiction."

"No, this is very much my jurisdiction. And you're not coming in this house until you are properly vetted and then cleared," she said, her arms over her chest, as she stood at Bonaparte's side.

"And who do you think you are to stop me?" he said. He looked over at the techs and said, "Get in there, and get your job done."

The techs looked at each other, looked at Angela, then shook their heads. "No, sir, we don't have her permission to enter."

"You don't need her permission."

"Well, actually they do," she said. "I have a legal and proper warrant for this property. Do you?"

He looked at her and said, "You do know we're on the same side, do you not?"

"That hasn't been determined yet. So get your own warrant," she said smoothly. Glaring at her, he took a few steps to the side and pulled out his phone. He had a conversation that nobody could hear, but they saw his frustration, evident as he stormed around in a circle, waving his hands, as he tried to get the answers he wanted.

Bonaparte looked at her and said, "Wow, I never realized being a deputy was this much fun."

She grinned. "Stick around, buddy," she said. "I could show you all kinds of fun times."

He stopped and looked at her. "Now, if only you meant that."

She looked up at him and said, "Hey, you're the one who promised me barbecued ribs and didn't deliver."

He groaned. "My poor ribs."

"Will they be okay?" she asked, a bit worried.

"They'll only get better," he said.

"Good," she said. "I doubt we'll get out of here any time soon."

"No, probably not," he said, "and we could have Stone wanting ribs now."

"Oh, no, no, no," she said, "then we definitely don't have enough. I know what that's like. Stone eats everything, including the kitchen sink."

Bonaparte burst out laughing at that, and all the techs stared at him sideways.

"We've got them flummoxed. You know that, right?" she murmured.

"Absolutely," he said, "but you're in the power of right."

"Well, I hope so," she said, "but I could lose that position very quickly."

"Got it," he said. "Let's just hope that doesn't happen."

She pointed at a plume of dust down the road. "From the speed that vehicle is traveling," she said, "what do you want to bet that's Stone?"

"Moving that fast, it's got to either be Stone or a helicopter," he said. "Hey, maybe Levi flew in a team."

"Nope, not a helicopter. Too bad," she said. "I'm due for a visit with all those guys."

"Hey, you could always come back with me afterward."

"That might be a good deal too," she said. "But when exactly is *afterward*?"

"When we get out of here," he said, smiling.

"Not sure that'll ever happen," she said.

"For you, you mean? Don't you get vacations?"

"Sure, I do. If I can take them," she said. "But, right now, I don't have anybody I can trust."

"What about your hospital security guard?" he asked.

"Well, he'll come on board as a deputy maybe," she said. "I was just doing a security check on him and getting some details, before I stepped ahead with that one, before all hell broke loose around here. Clearly he wouldn't be working as a security guard if he didn't have a decent background behind him, but I just hadn't quite gone that far."

"Any hesitation?" he asked.

She thought about it and shook her head. "No," she said, "he's a good person."

"And he's not involved in any of this mess?"

"Well, not to my knowledge," she said, "but that doesn't necessarily mean anything."

"Isn't that the truth," he said, happy that the plume of dust approached at an even faster clip.

She smiled and said, "I'll bet that's Stone, and he just caught sight of people being here, and he's trying to get here in time to lead the charge."

Bonaparte laughed. "He does like being out front."

"It's not often that he goes in the field now," she said. "Especially with his beautiful partner."

"Yeah, that's true enough too. Most of the guys are starting to be lazy asses, preferring to stay at home with their ladyloves."

"I bet they're not really lazy though," she said, looking at him in mock horror.

"No, that doesn't go down too well at the compound."

"Of course not," she said. "I know enough about Ice to understand there's no room for lazy on any ship she is running."

"That's true, though things are very different now that she has a baby," he said, but then he stopped and shook his head. "No, you know what? They're really not different at all. She's just as organized and on top of things as she always was. But there's a certain softness to her that wasn't there before."

"I'm guessing there's a lot more laughter for both of them," she murmured.

He nodded. "Exactly. For all of us actually."

"So, now that they've led the way, how many more babies are happening?"

Chuckling, Bonaparte said, "I suspect at least four or five in this next year or so." She looked at him in surprise. He shrugged. "What can I say? Anna and Flynn are pregnant."

"Wow," she said. "They're the ones with the rescue, aren't they?"

"Yep, they sure are," he said. "And a couple others, I hear."

Just then a vehicle came toward them. She watched as it approached. "What about Stone?"

"Not yet," he murmured. "But there was talk of it."

"But his wife is highfalutin, right?"

"It doesn't matter. She's actually pretty down to earth, when it comes to life in reality."

"That's good," Angela said. "Nothing worse than people with their head in the clouds, who just don't get it."

"No," he said, "and that's definitely not her problem."

When the large SUV blew through the gate, then took the corner superfast, she chuckled. "That is absolutely Stone."

The still-livid man in the suit on the phone watched as the vehicle screeched toward him. He turned and looked at her. "Now who the hell is that?"

"Oh, somebody who you probably need to meet," she said.

He glared at her. "And why the hell do I have to meet anybody?"

"Well, you're the one who's stepping on toes here," she said. He glared at her, not liking the expression on her face, she presumed. But she just smiled at him, as the vehicle slid to a stop, right in front of them. Immediately the crowd on the ground was covered in dust. "He always did like to make an entrance," she said affectionately.

Stone hopped out and strode forward. Taking one look at the two of them, he grinned. "Am I in time?"

One of the techs spoke up. "In time for what?"

"To bust a few heads," he said in a flat voice, as he turned to look at them. Bonaparte was huge and wide, and Stone, although shorter, was definitely no slouch when it came to size, so the techs immediately shrank back.

"We didn't do anything wrong," the lead tech said. "We're not even sure what the hell's going on."

"That's good," Stone said. "Just watch and learn." Walking over to Angela, he wrapped his arms around her, picked her up, and swung her around in a great big hug, like she was a two-year-old.

She shrieked with laughter, as he put her down again, and she gave him a big hug and a smoochy kiss on the cheek. "God, it's good to see you," she said.

"Way too long a time," Stone said. Then he reached over and smacked Bonaparte hard on the shoulder. "I see you've not missed any meals while you've been here."

She snorted. "Are you kidding? He's been holding ribs over my head all day," she complained in a mocking voice, knowing that the rest of the group gathered on the front lawn was staring at the three of them in amazement.

"That's not good," Stone said. "But I got to tell you, he does make the meanest ribs of anybody I've ever met."

She stared at him, then turned to look at Bonaparte. "Now that doesn't help matters at all," she snapped. "I really want to go home and get ribs."

"Hey, I'm all for it," Bonaparte said, "but we better deal with these guys first."

Angela turned, surveyed the crew, and realized that the two men who had come along with Stone had stepped out of the vehicle. They were currently pinning her irate suited adversary against the vehicle that he'd come in. "Who are they?"

"Two guys who investigate politicians," Stone said in a quiet voice. "Apparently they were on to some property issue going down here, and they were slowly building a case, but nobody realized just how much it had escalated and needed attention."

"Well, it sure as hell does," she snapped. "I don't want any of these guys in my town."

"No, I get it," he said. "By the way, Denver matched your bullet to the rifle and to fingerprints thereon for the uncle, who I hear is in the hospital."

"Good news, more evidence," Angela said, nodding at Bonaparte.

"And me?" Stone said, "I'm here as your reinforcement."

"Glad to have you too," she murmured. "Of course I'm glad to have you anytime. But today? Absolutely."

He crossed his arms, matching their posture, and stared out at the others. "Are these techs here harmless?"

"Absolutely," she said. "They're just caught in the middle." She looked over at them and said, "This should all be settled soon."

They looked at each other, some shrugging. Two of them had sat down on the ground by now and were stretched out with a cup of coffee from nearby thermoses.

She smiled at them. "I guess you get overtime either way, don't you?"

They just nodded. "Take as long as you want," said one of them. "Our base hours will be up soon, and we're more than happy to start into time and a half."

She chuckled. "At least something good will come out of today."

At that, the two men who came with Stone turned and whistled. Stone lifted a hand, and the three suits—the two good guys and the one bad guy—loaded the pushy man into his vehicle. She looked over at Stone. "What was that about?"

"Oh, that was just about prioritizing and realigning power," he said smoothly.

"So what resistance do we have now?"

"None."

One suit walked over and took a look at the three of them. "Angela?"

"If you mean, Sheriff Angela Zimmerman," she said in a cool voice, "yes, that's me."

He winced. "My apologies," he said. "I meant no disrespect."

"Good," she said, "then I don't have to brace you on it. Accidents can happen," she said generously.

He smiled at her. "That's very generous of you, considering the scenario. Thank you."

"You want to tell me what's going on here?" she asked.

"Let's just say somebody overplayed his hand, and he'll now be coming in with us to answer some questions."

"Excellent. I also have a jail full in town," she said, "and I'd really like to get those prisoners off my plate as well."

"Do you have both Ronnie and Johnny in custody?" he asked in surprise.

"I sure do, as well as Henry, one of their lackeys, and two women involved in this mess, though not necessarily by choice," she added. "Ronnie's uncle Hector is at the hospital. We're still looking for Frank though."

"We did get a phone call from the prosecutor," he said, "and their cases are interesting."

"They are," she said, looking at her watch. "I don't know if anybody has come to deal with Mama yet, but, she's going through chemo and radiation, and she can't be left alone much longer."

"Right," he said. "We'll head over to your station and pick up your prisoners. Hopefully we've got more of a team on the way."

"Good enough," she said, then frowned. "I'll need to come with you."

"We would appreciate it if this team is allowed to enter to collect all the evidence, and then it will all come back to Denver with us."

She frowned at that, studying him carefully.

"I know it's hard to believe," he said, "but we are the good guys."

She pulled out her phone and spoke as soon as Levi answered. "They came in with Stone, but nobody has identified themselves."

"Oh." The man immediately winced. Pulling out his wallet, he offered her his card and badge. She looked at it, not understanding the government tag on it.

She took a photo of the ID, sent it to Levi, then said, "Photo matches the person. His name is Robert Wagner."

"Yes, got the ID. That's one of the good guys," Levi said.

"Okay," she replied, "I'm holding you to it."

"No problem."

She put her phone away and faced Robert. "Levi says you're okay."

He nodded. "I'm grateful for Levi saying that," he said. "He's been very helpful to our team over the years."

"Yeah, that's Levi," she said. She looked at Stone and said, "Can you vouch for these two?"

"Hey, you just said Levi vouched for us," Robert replied.

"For you yes, but that doesn't mean I'm not against asking somebody else," she said, her voice low and hard. "I trust Stone too."

He looked over at the two men, then grinned and said, "Yeah, they're clear."

"Good enough," she said, addressing Robert again. "Then you can let your team come in and take the materials they need," she said, "but I want copies of everything found."

As Robert shook his head, she held up a hand and said, "Look. I'm not asking you. I'm telling you. We have an awful lot of crap going on in town right now and a lot of secondary cases that are related to yours. You decide, gentlemen, right now, before anyone else enters this residence." She looked from Robert to Stone.

Stone stared at Robert. It didn't take long.

"Agreed," Robert said.

And, with that, she stepped aside and let the forensics team enter. They all smiled at her as they headed in, and the last one whispered, "Now that was a class act."

"Hey, I didn't get to pull a gun at all," Bonaparte said. "Not my style."

"Not a problem," she said in a low voice. "I want to get back to the station."

"Problems?" Stone looked at her with a frown.

"Yeah, definitely."

Chapter 12

A NGELA LOOKED AT Bonaparte, nudged him, and said, "So?"

"It's all good," he said.

She turned to Stone and asked, "So do you want to join us for ribs after all this?"

"Well, I'll stay here and wait to make sure all this forensic evidence goes where it needs to," he said.

She frowned immediately. "Are you telling me that you're going back to Denver with them?"

He nodded. "Yeah, I'm not sure just what else is involved," he said, "but I don't like the idea of any of this going by the wayside."

She nodded. "Absolutely. We'll go back to the station, if you're okay to stay here and then transport the goods."

"No problem," he said. "I'll see you in a bit."

Angela and Bonaparte walked to his vehicle, hopped in, and headed to the sheriff's station. "Do you think the evidence is safe?" she asked.

"Nope," he said. "We're at a very dicey point in time. I didn't want to leave Stone alone, but I also don't like the idea of these guys collecting the prisoners on their own."

"Yeah, more bad guys against those two guys, unless they have a full crew with them or something."

"We don't know that they do," he said, picking up

speed, "or what else has happened in the meantime."

They were only a few minutes out, when she said, "I'm getting a really ugly feeling."

"You and me both," he said, as he whipped through the streets of town and came to a screeching stop in front of the station. She was out and running to the front door, before he even had the engine off. She knew he was right behind her because she heard his boots pelting the hardwood floor as she raced inside. She headed for the jail, and, when she entered the supposedly secure area, she stopped in shock.

"Oh, my God," she whispered. The two women were unconscious or dead on the ground. Considering they were still locked up in their cell, it didn't bode well for them. As Angela looked farther down the hallway, Henry appeared to be unconscious in his cell. Ronnie and Johnny were both missing. She raced in to check on Henry, but Bonaparte shook his head.

"He's dead."

She fished out the keys for the other cell, quickly unlocked it, and checked on both women. "They're both alive, she announced.

"I've got an ambulance coming," he said.

She headed for her security room. As soon as she got there, she checked the cameras and tapped the screen for Bonaparte to see. "Your two guys were taken out by somebody in the station already," she said in amazement. "Even with my deputy here."

"Yeah, speaking of that, where is your deputy?"

She stopped, stared, and swore. Picking up the phone, she called the neighboring sheriff and asked, "How good is your deputy?"

"What do you mean?" he said.

"I've got two prisoners missing, another dead, and two more knocked out."

And, with that, he started swearing. "Where's my deputy?" he roared.

"No idea," she snapped. "He apparently mentioned some friends he might bring over as backup."

"Ah, crap," he said. "Those two friends of his are both bad news. But that doesn't mean that he was too."

"We're checking now to see if he's lying unconscious somewhere."

"They might have taken him along," the sheriff said.

"This is just bad news," Angela said. "I have two government officials here, with yet another bad guy, coming to pick up the prisoners."

"And you're only missing the two?"

"I'm missing the two I don't want to be missing," she snapped. "Plus one dead that I don't want dead."

"Of course you are."

She hung up from him and immediately called Stone. "Watch your back," she barked. "My prisoners are missing. Plus I've got one dead prisoner, two unconscious prisoners, and my borrowed deputy is missing too."

"I'm on it," he said. "I'm out of sight and keeping guard on the forensic team right now."

"You need to," she said, "because I don't know whether my escaped prisoners are heading your way or if they're running."

"Probably both," he said, "but they need this evidence destroyed."

"I can't leave here until the ambulance arrives. Bonaparte is looking for the missing deputy. The security tapes go to about forty minutes ago, and then it's been unplugged."

"Of course," Stone said, "and that sounds like the deputy."

"I hate to say it, but that is quite possible. Now I've got to call the hospital to check on another prisoner I had under guard," she said. She hung up from Stone, dialed the hospital, and, when she got the administrator, she asked, "Is my security guard still on your patient?"

"Yes," said the man on the other end. "What's up?"

"We've had another break-in at the jail, and we have two prisoners missing. I need to verify that you guys are safe over there."

"Okay, I'm heading that way to check. How serious is this?" he asked, sounding worried.

"I have one dead prisoner, two unconscious, and a missing deputy, among other things," she said.

"Dammit," he said. "I'm almost to the ward."

"Hand me off to the security guard the minute you get there."

"Hang on." There was relief in his voice when he said, "I see him sitting there."

"Good. Let me talk to him."

He handed over the phone and said, "It's the sheriff."

"Hey, Sheriff. What's up?"

"We've got trouble, and it could be coming your way," she said urgently. "We had another break-in at the station. We've got a missing deputy, two unconscious prisoners, and one dead."

He whistled. "Wow, you really need some help."

"Yeah, well, I've got it now," she said. "This is a warning for you."

"And I appreciate it," he said. "We should be good. No trouble so far."

"Maybe," she said. "I'm not so sure about that, so I want you to be very careful. Johnny and Ronnie are both missing, and they could be tying up loose ends."

"Of course," he said in disgust. "Those two are just slippery."

"Absolutely," she said, "but listen. The deputy from Yorkston County could also be involved."

"Who, Harry? I thought I saw him in town."

"Yeah, Harry."

"Ah," he said. "Yeah, that makes sense. He's friends with that pair."

"What pair?" she asked.

"You know. Those brothers who run that one mechanics shop?"

"Yeah, are you talking about Floyd? Floyd and Roscoe?"

"Yeah. Turns out Harry is friends with both of them."

"And is that a problem?" She racked her brain, trying to think about the two of them. "My dealings with them have been petty crimes and small thefts and burglaries. They're basically lazy oafs, who don't work very much. Jesus, you'd think Deputy Harry would have better taste in friends."

"Yep, and they're looking to score big," he said. "Remember that part because it's always at the top of their minds too."

"Which means they're exactly the type Ronnie and Johnny would have used for one thing or another."

"I wouldn't be at all surprised," he said. "The trouble is, that deputy is likely to get killed over this, and he won't even see it coming."

"Thanks for the tip on that," she said. "We'll head down to the mechanics shop here in a minute."

"I've got this," he said. "You take care of that."

She hung up and, hearing the ambulance siren approaching, raced outside and led them to where the two women were. Within minutes, both were loaded up and headed for the hospital. She looked over at Henry. "God, he was too young for this."

"No," Bonaparte said. "He was old enough to know better."

"But he didn't care," she said.

He reached out a gentle hand, squeezed her shoulder, and said, "You can't save them all."

She looked up at him and took a long breath. "I know," she said. "At least my mind knows it, but my heart—" She shook her head.

He opened his arms, and, when she looked at him, he motioned for her again and said, "Come on."

She sighed, stepped into his embrace, and let herself be held for just a minute. "You do know that I'm the sheriff, right?"

"Yes, ma'am. And I know you're struggling to deal with calamity right now."

She squeezed him hard, and he let her. "You're like a bloody tree," she murmured.

"Hey," he said, "at least I put down roots and keep them there."

"Yeah," she said, with a smile.

He studied her for a moment. "So, when this is over," he said, "how would you feel about me sticking around for a few days?"

"I'd like that," she said. "Are you talking about officially or unofficially?"

"Well, you probably can't take much time off, not until you fill up your crew, so probably officially," he said.

"Meaning that, if I can't take days off, you'll stay and work?" she asked, with a laugh.

"It's probably the only way I can see you. Plus I'd like to make sure you have someone to back you up in the interim," he said.

"Well, it'll be up to me to hire a deputy." She gave him a sidelong look. "You want a job?"

He looked at her and then laughed. "Wow," he said. "I don't know about that. I don't think Levi would particularly like it."

"Well, Levi is a big boy," she said, with a smile. "Besides, he's been telling me how he had plenty of good men all the time."

"Which he does," he said. "And I'm one of them."

"Right," she said, with a sly grin. "God knows I could use a good man right now."

"Here I am," he said, with a big grin, raising his eyebrows.

She rolled her eyes. "Hardly."

"Why not?" he asked. "What's wrong with me? You know that I'm here for you," he said. "You know that I'm honest and trustworthy. I've got your back," he added. "What else do you need to know?"

"Well, I don't know much about your family or your kids." Then he launched into this long monologue of everything that he thought she needed to know, as she listened in astonishment. "So, are you serious?"

"Well, I won't say no," he said, cautiously eyeing her. "But you know something? There's an awful lot of spark or pizzazz or whatever you want to call it between us, and there's a hell of a lot to like about you."

"Really?" She smiled. "Oh, please."

"Really," he said, "and I agree. It's hardly the time or place but—"

"Right," she said, just as another ambulance arrived. "And this will be our deceased's wagon."

"Can they take him already?"

"Yes. Well …" Then she stopped, rolled her eyes, and said, "Maybe not." She called Stone. "Hey, how are your forensic guys doing?"

"They're still busy, why?"

"Well, I've got a body here," she said, "and it'll be connected to the case."

"Ah," he said. "Well, I might be able to send one or two your way."

"Only if they can," she said. "I know it'll take a full team to keep track of this."

"And what about the coroner?"

"Coming from Denver and should be here any minute, I hope," she said. "You've got a full house there that'll take a while. Unfortunately I'll be at it here for a while as well."

"Why don't you sit down in a chair and relax while you wait?" he said. "Nothing will happen quickly."

"Well, I want to get down to the hospital too," she said. "I not confident we won't have trouble there." Just then the coroner's vehicle arrived. "Well, I'm off," she said. "The coroner's here. I'll be heading to the hospital to check that out too."

"And what about Bonaparte?" he asked.

"He seems to think he needs to stick close."

Stone laughed. "Well, if he thinks that," he said, "you better let him."

"You mean, his instincts are good?"

"His instincts are some of the best," he admitted.

"You've got a lot going on and two missing jailbirds now," he said. "So, if Bonaparte thinks he needs to stick close, you better let him."

"Not only that, we have a mechanics shop to get to," she said. "I really could use a full contingent of experienced deputies right now."

"Well," he said, "I don't know who all to call in because I don't have anybody else local. Want me to come?"

"No," she said, "you handle that corner."

"Do you really think somebody will come here?" he asked thoughtfully.

"We can't take a chance. If the brothers can get that evidence away from you, we won't have a case."

"Good point," he said. "Okay, I'll stay here."

"Perfect," she said, "we're heading to the hospital in a minute." She disconnected the call with Stone to greet the coroner, then showed him what happened and said, "I've got it on video over here—or at least a little bit of it," she said. "I've got a handful of missing people too."

He shook his head. "This is bad business."

"It is, indeed."

"Aren't you up for reelection next year?"

"I am," she said, leveling him with a steady look. "A hell of a lot has been going on over the last few months, to the point that I have trouble keeping deputies."

"I heard about that," he said. "Bad business." He shook his head. "Go do your own thing," he said. "I've got this. I've got a team with me too."

"Where'd you get that from?"

"The two guys from Denver ordered it up."

"Interesting." She looked over at Bonaparte, who shrugged. "Any idea where those men are?" she asked the doc.

"I thought they were here," the coroner said.

"Did they call you here for this case?"

"Nope. Well, I don't know," he said. Then he stopped, frowned, and asked, "How did they know about this then?"

"That's what I'm asking," Angela said.

The doc said, "I was told something about a good chance of bodies before this was over."

"You come on *good chances* now?" she asked.

"No," he said, frowning. "And I didn't want it to be a wasted trip. I mean, I hate to say that I'm glad you have a body here, but, at the same time, they felt that they needed somebody like me here, just in case."

"Well, *just in case* certainly came true," she said. "But—"

He just waved at her. "I'll take care of this."

She nodded, looked over at Bonaparte, and the two of them headed for his truck. "Isn't that a little bizarre?"

"Yeah, though I know that Levi vouched for those two men. Honestly, if they were with Stone, that's just common sense to expect corpses."

She looked at him, startled.

He shrugged. "We may have a bit of a track record for leaving bodies in our wake."

She groaned. "Seriously, have you guys got that kind of rep?"

"Well, Stone certainly does," he said, with a big grin.

She phoned Stone, while Bonaparte drove. "Hey, the coroner was called by your two buddies."

"Yeah, we did that before you left," he said. "Is that a problem?"

"Well, the coroner doesn't usually come when we don't have a body."

"Yeah, but, sure enough, on a deal like this, there's usually a body," he said. "Everything's been a bit of a shit show so far. We thought it was a good idea."

"It's a good idea, and, of course, I do have one dead prisoner."

"See? Perfect."

"I doubt this guy appreciates being called out on a *possible*."

"Maybe, but he's just about to retire anyway, so he's always looking to get out of the office."

"If you say so." She shrugged. "It just seems pretty bizarre."

"Nothing more bizarre than a lot of the other stuff going on right now," he said.

"You got any action?"

"Uh, you mean in the five minutes since the last time you asked?" he asked in mock exasperation.

She groaned. "Sorry." She hung up to find they weren't that far from the hospital. She looked over at Bonaparte. "Did you mean it?"

"Mean what?" He looked at her in confusion.

"About sticking around for a few days."

"Absolutely. I'm here until you don't need me anymore," he said.

She smiled. "That's a pretty open-ended offer."

"It is," he said, "and I mean it."

She stared at him, feeling a warmth in her heart. "And that's really lovely to hear," she said. "It feels like a long time since anybody had my back."

"And that's not cool," he murmured. "And it's such a lovely back that I don't understand it."

She rolled her eyes. "Do you really expect a cheesy line

like that to work?"

"I don't know," he said, looking at her with interest. "Did it?"

She groaned. "Enough flirting."

"Nope," he said. "I'm French, so there's never enough flirting."

She sighed. "Okay, so you're gorgeous and have a smooth tongue—uh, *er*, wait. I meant you're, uh, ... artfully persuasive too." She could feel her face turning red, as she stammered.

"Ah, so you think I'm gorgeous," he said, with a chuckle, apparently letting her off the hook for her embarrassing gaffe.

She groaned. "Are you always this foolish?"

"Nope," he said, "just when we need to lighten the air a bit."

"It's not my usual method of handling stress," she said.

"Yeah, for a minute there, it kind of backfired," he said, with a chuckle. "Listen. In all seriousness, you care about everybody, and you're worried about everybody."

"Of course I'm worried," she said. "This is not how I planned the day out."

"No, but it's always a good thing to head off as much bad stuff as we can," he said. "If you think about it, we have enough problems going on right now."

"Maybe things will still be good at the hospital," she said, as they pulled up. She hopped out and strode into the building, and, with quick hard steps, headed for the ward, where her security guard was stationed.

He looked up and smiled. "It's all good here."

"You sure?" Looking at the prisoner, she nodded. "That doesn't look too bad," she said. "But I want you to step inside and sit in the room."

He looked at her in surprise and nodded. "I can do that. Are you really expecting a stealth attack?"

"I am," she said. "And remember. They'll want to prevent him from talking, and these guys are playing to the finish."

"That's good," he said. "So am I. And remember, Sheriff. I'm looking for a deputy position after this."

"We'll talk about it," she said, "but, for now, let's focus on keeping him alive." And, with that, she turned and headed back out again, Bonaparte keeping pace at her side.

"So where do you want to go now?"

"To an old mechanics shop," she said. "Not far, just over that way a bit."

He nodded, as they headed for the truck. She looked in that direction and said, "You know what? I think I'd like to walk."

"For the exercise?"

"No, that group is pretty wily."

"So who is it you're expecting to be there?"

"I really don't know, but it could be the whole freaking lot of them."

"Okay, good enough," he said. "Let's go."

As they headed around the corner, she looked at him and said, "You're just … so visible."

"Well, I can hardly shrink, but, if you want me to disappear, just say so."

"Well, that's impossible," she joked.

He looked at her, smiled, and said, "You might be surprised."

"Well, that's true," she said. "Maybe you should make yourself a little bit invisible."

"Done," he said, and she kept walking, soon realizing that she'd lost him. She didn't want to turn around and check where he was, blowing his cover, but she knew that he was out there, watching her back, and that was worth everything. Just the thought of him sticking around for a while and helping her out of this spot was worth so much too. He was a good man. She smiled, pulled her phone from her pocket as she walked, and sent him a message. **You're a good man.**

Does that mean we're still on for dinner?

We were never off.

Good. But that means we need a date afterward too.

A date? Why?

Sure, because this dinner is no longer a date.

Dinner was never a date! Her phone rang immediately, and she answered it, saying, "You're hilarious."

"Good," he said, "just keep your wits about you."

"My wits are about me," she said, looking around.

"So, it's a date then?" he asked.

"What's a date?" she replied.

"Us."

"The ribs?"

"No, of course not," he said. "That's not a date. That's just dinner. We've already been through this."

She groaned and said, "Fine, a date."

"In bed?"

"Hell," she said, "at this rate, maybe so."

He let out a soft *whoop* on the phone.

She laughed and said, "No, I don't go to bed on first dates."

"But the ribs will be a date."

"No," she said, "the ribs aren't a date. You just said so

yourself."

"Fine," he said, "after the ribs."

She groaned and said, "Enough." She pocketed the phone and quietly walked up to the front of the shop, where three vehicles were parked outside, all in worse shape than any mechanics shop could possibly pull back together again. Good thing this wasn't where her truck was being serviced.

As she walked up to the office door, she opened it enough to look inside. Nobody was in the office, which was nothing more than a small greasy little hole with blue shop towels on the counter and dirt all over the floor. Various cans of oil and other automotive fluids were stuck on a shelf, sitting beside a few other parts that looked like they'd been covered in dust and hadn't been touched in many years.

With nobody here, she opened the back door and stepped forward into the garage, seeing if anybody was around. And again found nobody. She studied the area, not liking anything about this. But she was here, and that was what she needed to do. She called out, "Anybody here?"

No answer. She walked through the garage area. Of the four bays, two hoists were in use, a car up on one, a truck on another, but it was down. The others were empty. Tools were scattered about, as if people had been working; then suddenly nobody was working. She knew a large parking area in the back was full of vehicles, used more as a pick-and-pull junkyard area for parts and scrap.

That's how the mechanics, another set of brothers, made their money as much as anything, and, so far, they'd kept it all reasonably clean and organized. And even though she'd been sheriff for a long time and knew they tended to waffle on the illegal side, they kept this operation on the right side of the law enough that she didn't have too much trouble with them. Which is why she hadn't considered them when this all went wrong—though now that she'd thought about it, they too were ripe for the picking.

As she walked through to the back door, she stopped at the exit and called out, "Anybody here?" And again was met with silence. With the back of her neck tingling, she stepped into the backyard toward the vehicles. As she gazed around, she slipped the back cover off her holster and walked forward ever-so-slowly.

"What's the matter, Sheriff?" asked a man off to the side of her. "What are you doing here?"

She turned to see one of the brothers, Floyd, standing there, wiping his hands on a blue rag.

"I came to see if you'd had any visitors," she said calmly. She looked him over, her gaze searching around the area.

"We always get visitors," he said. "What's that got to do with anything?"

"Your friend was in town, working for me today."

"Harry, yeah," he said. "We would stop by but decided against it."

"Well, that's a lie," she said calmly. "My cameras caught sight of you there." He stopped and glared at her, and she realized she was right. "You disconnected the electronics but not quite fast enough. We saw your vehicle pull up to the side." He started to swear. "So now that you're already ID'd as part of that mess," she said, "do you want to change your story?"

"No. Hell no," he said. "I got nothing to say."

"Good," she said. "Then you won't mind coming down to the station and having a little talk with me there then, will you?"

"I ain't going no place," he said. "I don't care what kind

of a sheriff you think you are. You're just a pair of tits and a piece of ass," he said, "and you ain't got no jurisdiction over me."

"Says you," she replied, with a smile. "In fact, I have as much law as anybody."

"Nah," he said, "not for long anyway. There's new law in town."

"Oh, you mean Ronnie and Johnny? The ones you broke out of jail? You realize you committed a felony by killing Henry at the same time?"

He stopped, looked at her, and said, "Henry?"

"Or did you not realize that you hit him hard enough that he's dead?"

He shook his head. "No, no, no, no, no. Henry was alive when we left."

She smiled. "Yeah, that's what you say now. But he was dead when we got there, so he died during your little escapade, freeing Ronnie and Johnny."

"No way. No, no, no," he said. "You won't pin a murder charge on me."

"Well, it's definitely a murder that happened while you were committing a crime," she said. "And you know that the law really doesn't care about what part you played in the murder, so you'll be going down for that too."

"Hell, no," he snapped. "This ain't got anything to do with me."

"You're a little late to be protesting," she said. "So, where are the rest of them?" He just glared at her. "I asked," she said, stepping forward, "where are the rest of them?"

Shoving his chin out at her, he said, "None of your fucking business."

"All right, have it your way," she said, eyeing him carefully. "So, will you come in and talk to me, or will you resist arrest?"

"I'm not talking to you," he sneered, "and you ain't making me either."

"Well, I could," she said, studying him, "but I don't have to."

"And why is that?" he asked, glaring at her.

"Because that guy, behind you, he won't have a problem doing it for me."

Floyd spun around, and there was Bonaparte, towering over him. Floyd gulped, went to grab something in his back pocket. Bonaparte clocked him one in the face, his jaw like butter, and he crumbled to the ground.

"Jesus, I hope you didn't kill him," she said.

"Not unless something's wrong with that jaw of his." Bending down to check him, Bonaparte then stood, shaking his head. "No, he's got a strong pulse."

"Good," she said, "but I don't have a good feeling about this."

"Neither do I," he said, studying the junkyard. "A lot of vehicles are here."

"Not only that," she replied, "he's also got a crusher in the back."

"We better start there," Bonaparte said, and he loped in the direction she pointed. Leaving Floyd tied up on the ground, they headed into the back. Sounds of machinery started up. She pointed off to the side, and the two of them raced as fast as they could in that direction. When she got there, a black vehicle with heavily tinted windows—the same one they'd seen earlier, delivering the crooked guy in a suit from Denver—was up on the deck, being lifted by the crane for the crusher. She immediately ordered the guy operating the crane to stop, but he just kept on going. "Looks like Floyd's brother, Roscoe."

"We have to get up there," Bonaparte said.

"Do you really think somebody's in the vehicle?"

"We can't take the chance," Bonaparte yelled, and he was already climbing the crane. It looked like Roscoe caught sight of him and tried to shift the angle of the crane, but that wouldn't stop Bonaparte, who was climbing fast. By the time he was at the top, the car had been sent over to the crusher. But with Bonaparte's gun pointed at Roscoe, he stopped. Immediately Bonaparte took control of the crane and slowly lowered the vehicle to the ground. She raced over to the vehicle, opened up the trunk, and found the two men Levi had sent down with Stone. Robert was alive and awake, staring at her in shock.

"Well, damn," she said, "that was a little too close." She helped him out of the trunk; then she reached in and checked his partner. "He's alive," she said, with relief.

"Yeah, I don't know about the two guys in the front seat though," Robert said.

She walked around and checked inside the vehicle. Sure enough, the corrupt Denver guy, who had tried to take over her operation, lay here, a bullet in his head. Beside him was the dead deputy on loan, Harry. "Damn," she said. "This just keeps getting better and better."

"Well, at least the Denver guy talked a lot while they had us," Robert said. "We just have to find the two behind it all."

"You mean, Ronnie and Johnny?" she said. "Those two have become such a pain in my ass."

"Yours and mine both," Robert said.

"That's all right," said another man, joining them.

Hearing a rifle locking into position, she turned to see Ronnie and Johnny standing there, each holding a weapon. "Wow," she said, "you guys have turned into quite a pain."

"No, that's you," Ronnie said. "All you had to do was let these guys get crushed, and it would have been a piece of cake."

"Nope," she said, "you would have just kept on coming."

"Absolutely," he said. "That's who we are."

"This is all about money," she said. Noticing Robert, now at her side, trying to stand up straight, she reached over and gave him a hand.

"This is a hell of a situation." Robert stared at the two brothers. "I just don't get it," he said. "After all this, why do you still expect to get away with it? Ronnie, you do know that we got all your electronics from your house, right?"

Ronnie shrugged and Johnny cackled. "Why wouldn't we get away with this?" Johnny said, the bandage on his shoulder visible. "We'll take out you three, plus that mammoth you brought into this deal. I still owe that asshole for the bullet in my shoulder."

"It was hardly a bullet," she said calmly. "It was barely a flesh wound, as I recall."

As she spoke, she wondered what the hell Bonaparte was doing. But she just had to trust that he was up there and knew firsthand what was going on. She didn't see how the evil brothers behind this could not know Bonaparte was in the crane, but she saw no sign of their recognition. So far, everything had been going in a completely crazed way anyhow. "This is all about money, and now you're here, ready to kill how many more people?"

"It doesn't matter how many," Ronnie said. "After the

first one it's easy. We've killed probably six so far, so what's another four or five?"

She shook her head. "And, with the local authorities and now the FBI on to your plan, you really expect to get out of this?"

"Will you?" he asked derisively. "You do realize who's holding a gun on you, right?"

She nodded. "Absolutely I do," she said, "but is that supposed to make a difference to me? I still have a job to do."

He frowned at her. "I don't get it," he said. "How the hell are you not worried?"

"Because you're still just punks," she said wearily. "You're nothing but petty-ass punks."

"Nothing petty ass about us, bitch," Johnny said, lifting the rifle in her direction.

The man she was helping to stay upright, who's name she had already forgotten, looked at Johnny. "You don't have to shoot her, man."

"Oh, yeah? Well, I do," he said. "I absolutely do. And don't worry. You'll get a bullet too. Because you're the one who tracked down our buddy here and messed up this deal. He was the one pushing things through for us."

"It's not that simple though," Robert said. "You don't get things pushed through on just one person's vote. Did he tell you that he could?"

"Hell yes, he said he could get it done," Ronnie said.

"Well, I'm sure he was trying his best for you," Robert said, "but voting still had to happen. Engineering designs still had to be drawn up, environmental planning processes done, and all kinds of shit *still* had to happen."

"And he would have made it happen," Johnny said. "We

know him. We know what he's like and what he's done before."

"Maybe so, and now we'll have to sort through his wretched life to see how much other shit he has pulled."

"Yeah, well, he's dead already, so I don't think it matters."

"Yet you killed him, and now you can't get your deal to go through," Angela said.

"There'll be somebody else," Ronnie said confidently. "Every time we go to a new state, somebody's there who's willing to take a payout instead of being an honest, upstanding citizen," he said, with that mocking tone of his. "You should try it sometime."

"Well, I would say, you should try being an honest citizen for once, but apparently you're just full of shit," she said. She had gotten her hand free and clear, but no way could she shoot both of them at the same time. She looked over at the man she'd been helping and said, "Sit down again, Robert," she said, then propped him up against the rim of the trunk. As she turned around, she pushed him in and fired at Ronnie, then rolled under the vehicle. Robert collapsed into the trunk, neatly folding back inside again, as, from the ground, Angela propped up and went to take another shot, only to see the crane swinging around, knocking Johnny to the ground. She bounded to her feet and ran over and checked on the first one, but her shot was true. She'd taken Ronnie out with a headshot.

As she walked over to the other body, her handgun still out and at the ready, she realized that Johnny was dead too. She looked up at Bonaparte and gave him a thumbs-up. She walked over to Robert and helped him back out again. "You okay?"

He took a long deep breath. "I am now," he said, "and again I owe you thanks."

"Well," she said, "just make sure you make good use of your life at this point."

He laughed. "I've already spent a lifetime putting criminals away. I'm not sure what else I can do."

"I'm sure you can find more bad guys to topple," she said, "but let's make sure this mess comes to a nice neat crisp end."

"A lot of it'll have to stay under wraps," he warned.

She winced. "That's too bad," she said. "I get that, in some related cases, it's necessary, but I really want to make sure all the perpetrators in this mess get caught."

"What about your deputies?"

"Well, I've got a security guard I'll deputize, and I have Bonaparte here," she said, "although he won't stay long-term."

"That's too bad," Robert said, looking up, as Bonaparte climbed down the crane.

"Yeah, except Levi wouldn't be very happy with me, if I were to steal one of his guys," she said, with a quick grin.

"Is he one of Levi's men?"

"He is," she said. "Levi was good enough to send him to help me."

"Levi's a great guy, and he has a top-notch team."

"Exactly. So, when I got into trouble, they were the first ones I called on."

"Good choice," he said. "That makes sense to me."

She smiled and nodded, as Bonaparte hopped down and finally joined them. "What about your buddy Roscoe up there?" she asked.

"I've got him hog-tied. He's not going anywhere."

"Good," she said. "We better go check on Floyd. That gives us two alive, plus the older one in the hospital. I think he's the evil brothers' uncle Hector."

"Yeah, we've got a few bits and pieces to pick up around town yet," Robert said. "But, other than that, Sheriff, you've done a pretty damn good job of cleaning up your town."

She smiled. "I have, haven't I? Too bad the locals won't believe me."

"Oh, I think they will," Robert said. "You'll get the credit for this. I'll make sure."

"I appreciate that," she said. "After all, it is an election year."

He burst out laughing. "I can't see that anybody will have a problem with this."

"You'd be surprised," she said. "A lot of folks here didn't want to see a woman elected in the first place."

"Well, maybe this will change their minds," he said. "Nobody else could have handled it better."

As she looked over at Bonaparte, he wrapped an arm around her shoulders.

Robert smiled and said, "That was a pretty impressive move she made, wasn't it?"

Bonaparte smiled and said. "That's one way to put it."

As IT WAS, Bonaparte was still adjusting to his own slamming heart after seeing her caught up behind those two rifles. It had been all he could do to get to the controls and to get that damn crane over them, without them really focusing on it. But once she dumped Robert back into the trunk and made her move taking out one brother, Bonaparte had had his chance.

After they'd further secured Floyd, who was just beginning to stir, and after Robert stated he was awaiting another crew to tie up things at the garage, Bonaparte and Angela started walking.

"Now what?" Bonaparte asked.

"We'll be a couple more hours here," she said, rotating her neck and head. "Plus there's about a million reports to write up."

"I think the sheriff needs a day off," he said.

"Well, it won't happen any time soon," she said.

"Can you work from home tomorrow?"

She thought about it. "Maybe," she said. "I'm sure my office will still be a crime scene for the forensic team to process, regarding this whole mess with my prisoners."

"That's fine," he said. "We can still cook the ribs when we're done."

"Yeah, what about Stone?"

"We can invite him, if you want. We'll cook the steaks too, if we need more food."

"That'd be nice," she said.

Pulling out his phone, Bonaparte punched in a number and said, "Stone, we're pretty well in the clear. How are you doing?"

Stone laughed and said, "It's been quiet here."

"Well, that's good," he said. "We've seen enough action for quite a while. I'm trying to drag her back home again, but it's gonna be a few hours before we're free and clear. Are you up for ribs tomorrow, or are you leaving right away?"

"I'm heading into town with the evidence," he said.

"Right, I forgot about that. You sticking around town for long, or will you be done?"

"I'll need to come back tomorrow," Stone said.

"Good, come for a barbecue then."

"Those ribs?"

Yeah," he said, "the ribs."

"I'll be there," he said enthusiastically.

Pocketing his phone, Bonaparte said, "Ribs it is, with Stone tomorrow."

"Perfect," Angela said.

"I promised, and I mean to deliver too," he said. With a grin, he wrapped an arm around her shoulders and said, "Let's head back to the station, leave these guys to their work."

"I don't know if we should leave Robert alone to handle this," she said. "We still don't know who all is involved in this scheme."

Bonaparte nodded, then pulled her away from the scene behind him, and said, "Absolutely. I spoke with Levi, and he's got tracking on all known associates of Ronnie and Johnny. Oh, and our Hummer guy, he has ties to another mob family, as well as to the evil brothers and their own Gapone mob family. Maybe the Gapones got their seed money from for these real estate ventures from the other family. Anyway, Levi gave me the all clear. So Robert will take care of cleaning up this mess here at the garage."

"Oh, good," she said. "If we can leave then, that would be lovely."

When they arrived at the station, she realized it was still full as well. She looked at everybody working away. "You know what? Stone told me to relax, that it would be a while. So I may as well just go home."

"You do that," the coroner said. "I think you've been involved in enough chaos today."

"Yeah, about that," she said. "You probably don't know

yet that you've got another crime scene."

He looked at her. "How many bodies?"

She winced and said, "Four, that I know of."

He just stared at her, his jaw dropping.

"I only took out one," she said, her hands up, palms showing.

And Bonaparte chimed in, "And one for me. But seems the bad guys took out the other two."

Shaking his head, the coroner finally closed his mouth, then said, "Well, I was hoping to get some sleep tonight, but I guess that will have to wait."

"Yeah, me too."

"Go," he said, "both of you. Get the hell out of my world," the doc said. "You make too much work for me. I'm trying to retire. Remember?"

"And here I thought you came as a special deal anyway," Angela teased.

"I did," he snapped in mock anger. "But that doesn't mean I wanted to push my retirement back twenty years. Do you have any idea how much paperwork this involves?"

She smiled and said, "Yeah, I have a fair amount back-logged myself. May I just say that your participation is really appreciated."

"Get lost, you two," he said, with a muffled chuckle.

"Will do."

And, with that, Bonaparte realized it was finally time for them to leave. "It's also dark," he said, "and it's been a shit show all day. Let's go home and recharge."

"I can get behind that," she said.

Chapter 13

OUTSIDE, ANGELA HOPPED into the vehicle and stared at the steering wheel in front of her.

He opened the door, looked at her, and said, "Move over."

She protested immediately. "I can drive."

"Doesn't matter if you can or not," he said, "I'm driving."

She glared at him but didn't have enough energy to fight him on this. The farther away from the action they got, the more she had shock setting in.

Pulling out of the parking lot at the sheriff's office and pointing the truck toward her place, Bonaparte said, "Let's go home."

"Yeah," she said, "that's a great idea. At least it's home for me."

"You've got a hell of a place out there," he said.

"Well, if you'd stick around," she murmured, "you could spend some time there."

"And that's very tempting," he said.

"Ha," she said. "Everybody is after me for my property."

"Hell no," he said, "I'm after you for your body."

Totally caught off guard, she burst out laughing.

He grinned at her. "See? You're feeling much better already."

"Oh, my God," she said, "you can't say things like that to me."

"Why not?"

She just shook her head, the mirth still bubbling up. "I think I'm too exhausted," she said. "Suddenly everything is making me laugh, even when it's not funny."

"Hey, that was very funny," he said in an injured tone.

She rolled her eyes. "You're such a comedian."

"I can be," he said. "But don't forget that I'm also loyal and true and trustworthy."

"So are puppies."

At that, he burst out laughing too.

By the time they made it to her place, she knew, by the way she was feeling, that she must look like death warmed over. When he pulled up to the front, she hopped out and immediately sagged.

"Are you hurt?" he asked, as he raced around to her side.

She shook her head. "No," she said, "I'm just—"

"Exhausted," he said. "You're physically and emotionally exhausted." He led the way to the front door and took her inside, the dogs milling around them, subdued, as if worried about Angela too. Bonaparte motioned toward her bedroom. "Just go get some sleep."

"I should have a shower," she said.

"Okay, if you got the energy, then do it," he said. "You'd probably sleep better. Just don't let all those bodies and this day take over your mind," he said, "because then you'll never sleep."

"I know," she whispered. "I was trying to hold all that back for now."

"You'll have to deal with it, but, if you could get some rest first, it would be better," he said. "No way you kill someone in the line of duty and walk away from that without feeling some reaction."

"We *should* feel a reaction," she murmured.

"Absolutely," he said quietly. "That's what makes us different from the bad guys, who feel nothing but maybe power and revenge. Come on. Let's get you upstairs." He helped her to her bedroom.

"I'll be fine from here," she said.

"Good," he said. "If I don't hear you moving around in the shower, I'm coming in after you."

She smiled. "That sounds like an excuse," she teased.

"I don't need an excuse," he said, "but, right now, if I were to take you to bed," he said, "you might fall asleep on me, and my ego couldn't handle that."

She broke out laughing again. "I don't know what it is about you," she said, "but, every time I'm around you, I end up smiling."

He grinned and said, "That's a good thing."

"Maybe," she said. "It seems like there hasn't been a whole lot of laughter in my life for a while."

"We'll change that now," he said.

She slowly made her way into the bedroom, closing the door between them. Stripped down, she headed for the shower. Once she was alone and under the hot water, she just leaned against the wall and let it pour all over her. When there was a knock on the bathroom door, she lifted her head and said, "I'm fine."

"Are you sure?"

She could hear the worry in his tone. She shut off the taps and poked her head around the corner of the shower curtain. "Really, I'm fine," she said. "I'm just ..."

When she let her voice trail off, he poked his head

around the door, nodded, and said, "As long as you're okay."

She smiled. "I'll be fine."

He closed the door and said, "I'm putting on coffee."

"That sounds good. Bring me a cup, if you don't mind."

"Will do."

She got out, and, instead of getting dressed, she put on an oversized T-shirt and baby-blue underwear, then crawled into bed, a hairbrush in her hand. "What a day," she whispered to herself. He knocked a few minutes later, and she called out, "It's open."

The door moved jerkily open, as he had used his foot to prod it, and she noted he carried a tray. She smiled, as he brought in a cup of coffee. "Do you really think I need coffee?" she asked, leaning her head back.

"You asked for it," he said.

She nodded. "I'm looking for the comfort of the hot drink, I suppose. And I highly doubt that the caffeine will stop me from sleeping tonight." He placed the tray gently on her lap, and he'd made a simple sandwich for her as well. "And food," she said. "Wow, you're a keeper."

"I am, at that," he said, with a smile.

She lifted one half of the sandwich and chewed gently. "Gosh, I didn't realize how hungry I was," she muttered.

"We haven't had anything all day," he said.

She nodded tiredly and finished the sandwich in about eight bites. Picking up the coffee, she sat here, hugging the warm cup, sipping it, as she huddled under the blankets.

"And now," he said, as he removed the tray and put it on the floor, "you need to crash."

"I know," she said. She put down her cup and shifted, so she was curled up under the covers, and pulled her pillow up under her neck. "You okay to stand watch?"

He reached out a gentle finger across her cheek and whispered, "Over you? Always."

But she didn't hear him. She was already out.

BONAPARTE QUICKLY TOOK the tray downstairs and left the bedroom door open, so he could hear her. He wasn't sure what she was like, but, for most people, after shootings and all the stress and adrenaline related to that, it was rare to sleep very deep. It wasn't long before he heard her crying out, tossing and turning. He raced upstairs and soothed her, until she was calm and relaxed again.

Leaving her for a few more minutes, he walked to his room and had a quick shower. With clean boxers and jeans on, he went to check on her. As he stepped inside her bedroom, she opened her eyes and stared at him, jolting awake.

He winced. "Sorry, I was just checking to see if you're okay," he said.

She looked at him in surprise and yawned. "I'm feeling much better."

"That's good," he said. "Go to sleep and really sleep this time."

"Working on it," she said; then she rolled over. Before he stepped out, she asked him, "What are you doing?"

"I just had a shower," he said, "so I'll try to get some rest too."

She patted the bed. "Just stretch out here then."

"Dangerous idea," he murmured, but she waved her hand to that.

"I'm too damn tired."

"What makes you think I am?"

"I'm trusting you," she said. "Besides, you want someone a little more with it. You said so yourself."

He smiled and said, "Absolutely," then stretched out on top of the bed.

"Don't you want a blanket?" she asked.

"I'm fine," he said. "Just rest."

She yawned again and crashed. He waited until she'd fallen asleep; then he got up, checked outside to make sure it was all safe. He was operating on instincts at this point. When his phone buzzed, he found a text from Levi. Bonaparte called him back and quickly gave Levi the latest update, but it wasn't long before Angela started whimpering again. Bonaparte finished the call, then went back and checked on her. Finally he decided to just lie down beside her and be a tortured soul for the night, pulling her into his arms. As soon as he had her up tight against him, she relaxed. He murmured, "Sleep now.

"Bonaparte?"

"Yep, it's me."

She smiled and rubbed her cheek against his chest. "Thank you."

"You're welcome," he said. "Just sleep."

"It's been a tough day," she said, yawning.

"It has," he replied, then waited for her to drop back to sleep again.

She did, but it didn't last. She kept waking up, going under, and waking up. Finally she sat up and looked at him and said, "It's a pretty rough night."

"That's because you won't quite go under," he said.

"I can't," she said. "I'm too restless." She yawned and flattened out again on the bed.

"Try to sleep," he said.

"No, you sleep."

He looked at her and started to chuckle. "What difference will that make?"

"I won't feel guilty."

He stared at her in surprise. "Why would you feel guilty?"

"Because it's always been me looking after everybody else," she said quietly. "Now I feel like I can't sleep because you're here, looking after me."

He pulled her down, until she was half lying on top of him, and said, "How about we both sleep?"

She looked up at him, smiled gently, and said, "I think I can handle that." She dropped her head on his chest, and it wasn't long before he heard a gentle rumbling, as her breathing moved in and out. He cuddled her close, wondering how he'd ended up in this situation. But, of course, it was all due to Levi.

And thinking about all that Levi had said, Bonaparte realized he owed him a debt. He hadn't expected to be here and wasn't even sure where things would go in the future, but he knew he wanted to find out. Even if that meant he'd be commuting back and forth for a while, while they figured it out.

Just when he thought she was sound asleep, she asked, "Will you commute back and forth?"

He chuckled lightly.

"We can't have a relationship if you're living several states away."

He nodded, completely stunned because she was mimicking his thoughts. "Is that what you want?"

"Well, I want some time to see what we have," she said.

"Do we have something?"

Immediately she opened her eyes and looked up at him.

He stared into the deepest, darkest, bluest eyes he'd ever imagined.

"Are you saying we don't?"

He reached up, stroked her lips, and said, "Well, I was hoping."

"You're just a little gun-shy."

"No," he said, "just had a bit of a bad experience and all that."

"Right," she said, snuggling in again. "Gun-shy."

He let out a deep, long breath. "Not exactly."

"Good, then you'll travel back and forth until you decide what you want."

"Why is it me traveling back and forth?" he teased, protesting.

She opened her eyes, stared at him, and said, "Would you really ask me to leave this property?"

He shook his head and whispered, "No, never."

She smiled, and it was breathtaking. "See?" she said. "So you'll have to fly back and forth."

He burst out laughing. "What's weird is that I was laying here, thinking just that."

She nodded and cuddled up closer. "We're already thinking the same."

"We don't really—" Then he stopped.

"What? We don't really know each other? We haven't spent any time together? What were you going to say?"

"I was about to say something along those lines, but then I stopped myself because it's straight-out foolishness," he said.

"I know," she said. "I don't understand what we have here yet, but I thank Levi for sending you."

"Don't you dare tell him that," he said. "It will just make him arrogant."

"He already is," she said, with a grin.

"Well, that's because he's damn good at what he does."

Angela had never really believed in love at first sight, and she had to admit that Levi had sent a picture of Bonaparte earlier, like quite a bit earlier, and she'd been staring at it for a long time. She already felt like she knew a lot about him but didn't want to say anything to him because it felt stalker creepy. But just having him here with her as they were, it felt so right in a way that she hadn't felt in a very long time. "I know. But do you know they were trying to send you to me one year ago?"

"Nope, I did not."

"Yeah, he told me about how he had his eye on you and how you were perfect for me."

"He what?" Bonaparte said in shock.

"Yep, but you were being stubborn and not listening. I'm sure glad you're not being stubborn anymore."

He didn't know what else to do, so he laughed and laughed.

Popping up, she sat on her knees and looked at him. "See? We laugh a lot."

"We do that," he said, staring at her in amusement.

"Now the question is," she said, "will we decide to move forward."

"Well, I am ready," he said. "What will it take to make your decision?"

"Ribs," she said. He stared at her and blinked. "Your ribs," she said. "It'll all depend on your ribs." He stared at her, afraid she was serious, and then she burst out laughing herself. "The look on your face," she said, as she rolled over onto her back.

Immediately he flipped over, so he was on top of her and said, "Yeah, what about the look on my face?" She looked up at him, and her breath caught in the back of her throat. He nodded. "Did you ever see that look from me earlier?"

"No," she said quietly. "That look was well hidden."

"That well-hidden look," he said, "was because we were at work."

"And we're not at work now," she said, wiggling beneath him.

This time his breath caught. "Exactly."

She smiled and wiggled again.

"You are so asking for trouble."

"Nope," she said, "I'm asking for loving. A good old-fashioned loving. Between two people who care about each other and maybe, just maybe, have something that they're both prepared to work on."

"God," he whispered fervently, "I really like the sound of that." Lowering his head, he kissed her for the first time.

Chapter 14

W HEN BONAPARTE FINALLY lifted his head from their
first kiss, Angela was starved for air. But, at the same
time, so much heat rumbled through her, as she whispered,
"That was very nice. Really very nice."

"*Nice?*" he said in mock outrage. This time he delivered
a passionate punch that had her gasping.

She shuddered in his arms. "It won't be just you that's in
a rush," she muttered. "No way you can kiss me like that and
leave me hanging."

Chuckling, he bent over and whispered, "I thought we
had time though."

"Nope," she said. "I'm tired." He looked at her in surprise and asked, "So, do you want to wait?"

"Hell no," she said. "This is the best cure for sleepless-
ness ever."

"And yet you just said you're tired."

"And you'll make me supertired and relaxed," she said,
"and then I'll sleep." And she threw her arms around his
neck and tugged him down to her. "But more than that," she
said, "we have something that I just don't want to let go of."

She pulled him to her, and this time she kissed him back
with all the passion she could feel being restrained inside. As
tired as she was, there was just no energy to even try to block
any of it. She felt herself letting go, like she hadn't ever

remembered letting go. Before she even had a chance to take note of it, she was stretched out on the bed, and her clothes were on the floor, along with his boxers and jeans. She scooted over, so there was more room for him, but he held out his hand, to stop her from moving, his gaze wandering all over her long, lean pink-toned skin.

"Like what you see?" she asked, stretching her head up.

"Jesus," he said, "you're stunning."

"No," she said, "I'm not voluptuous. I'm long. I'm lean and a little sparse in spots," she said.

"You're perfect," he said, holding out a halting hand again. "Absolutely gorgeous."

Smiling, she dropped herself onto her back, opened up her arms, and said, "In that case, show me." He lowered himself, and she was surprised at the gentleness of this giant, as he held her close in his arms. He just held her for a long moment, and, when she looked up and saw the emotions on his face, her heart was breaking. She reached up with a gentle finger. "You okay?"

"I am," he whispered. He stopped and then shrugged and said, "Just a little overcome at the moment."

"In that case," she said, "I understand entirely." He lowered his head once more, this time with a gentle tenderness, with a level of emotion she didn't really understand. Almost as if she were being held, like a glass rose, and he was afraid she might break. But it wasn't that physically he was holding back, more like he was handling the emotions rising in him. She wrapped her arms around him. "This is us," she said. "This is what we make of it. So let's make something good."

He bent to kiss her, and this time it was a ride that neither one of them could stop. Passion flowed freely, as heat built and surrounded them in a glorious aftermath. When he finally lay trembling in her arms, her body flushed and with a sureness she hadn't expected to feel, she held him close and whispered, "Now get some rest."

"Only if you rest first."

She smiled, curled up in his arms, and said, "Absolutely." And the two of them soon dropped off to sleep. When she woke the next morning, she was still in his arms, the way they had been as they fell asleep.

He looked at her and asked, "You okay?"

"Never better," she whispered. She slowly sat up, looked around at the room, and said, "That was one of the best nights I've ever had," she whispered, then leaned over and kissed him tenderly.

He stroked a lazy hand up her back and asked, "Are you in a hurry?"

"Well, I'm sure there's a million messages, half a million reports, and a whole pile of other things that need my attention," she said.

"Maybe," he said, "but something else does too." He took her hand and slid it down across his body to the very large erection waiting for her.

She burst out laughing and said, "By the way, there's another thing I like to do on my acreage."

He looked at her and asked, "What?"

"Later," she said, while the two made love again. When they finished, the two of them were completely sated, each exhausted and panting on the bed.

"That's a hell of a way to wake up," he said, groaning.

"It is. And since you made coffee last night," she said, "I'll make coffee now." She bounded out of bed and headed to the doorway.

He called out, "Are you getting dressed?"

She looked at him, shrugged, and said, "Actually I was thinking about a dip in the pool."

He sat up, smiled at her, and said, "I would absolutely love that."

"You know what?" she said, as she leaned against the door, completely at home in her nudity. "I'm afraid I'm falling in love with you."

"Is that a problem?" he asked, his dark gaze on her.

She wasn't sure how to say it, but she decided to toss it out there anyway. "Did you know that Levi sent me your photo one year ago, around the same time he wanted to send you out here?"

His eyes widened. "What?"

"He did, and that's something I've kept just in the back of my mind. For maybe one day."

"Wow," he said, "that is a complete shock."

"Does it bother you?"

"Hell no," he said. "I wasn't nearly ready a year ago," he said, "but I'm more than ready now." He smiled, threw off the covers, then hopped up and came toward her. "How about that swim?"

"Sure," she said. "Sounds like a perfect idea."

"You don't expect anybody to come out there while we're skinny-dipping?"

"Not unless you've got Stone on the way."

He checked his jeans, pulled his phone from the pocket, and checked his messages. "Dang. Stone is on his way."

She looked at him and rolled her eyes. Walking to her dresser she pulled out a pair of panties. Then, on to her closet, she pulled out a sundress and said, "Clothes it is then." As soon as she was dressed, she said, "You better get something on too."

"He'll still know."

She looked at him and smiled. "I don't care. Do you?"

"Are you kidding? I'd be happy to show the rest of the world what we have."

"Are you sure?"

"Very sure," he whispered. Then he leaned forward and said, "And the sooner they find out, the better, because we are together. Hopefully, for the rest of our lives."

She reached up and kissed him gently on the lips. "That sounds perfect for me." As they separated, she heard a vehicle honking at the driveway gate. "And here's Stone," she said. "Time to start the day."

And she raced down the stairs, laughing, unsure if she had ever seen such a great day before. The morning was bright. The birds were singing, and her body hummed with joy. As she flung open the front door to welcome Stone, she realized she'd never been happier. It was a perfect day.

Epilogue

NOAH WILKERSON WALKED into Levi's kitchen and sat down.

"Hey, Noah. Even your buddy Bonaparte is hooked up now, isn't he?" Levi asked.

Just then Bonaparte walked into the kitchen. "What's this? I heard my name, didn't I?"

"Yeah, how is Angela doing?"

"She's doing amazing," he said, with a big grin.

Noah stared at him. "I haven't seen that smile on your face before."

"Hey," he said, "you haven't met Angela."

Noah laughed. "Nope, but I do hear that you were pretty resistant to the idea before you went out there."

"I sure was, but she changed my mind pretty damn fast."

Noah looked over at Levi, just as Ice appeared. "So, you guys are running quite the matchmaking service, it seems."

"Sometimes it works out that way," Ice said, with a smile. "You interested?"

He thought about it, shrugged, and said, "Well, if you can find me a partner like the ones you've found for these guys, maybe," he said. "I can't say I've really been thinking about it though."

"Of course not," Ice said, her smile growing bigger. "Nobody really thinks about it, unless they've been trying for a long time."

"Nope, not me. I broke up about a year ago from a long-term relationship and haven't really found anybody interesting since."

"What broke it up, Noah?" Bonaparte asked.

"She wanted a family, and, in the four years we were together, apparently she couldn't conceive. So she decided she wanted to change the herd sire." They all just stared at him, and finally he shrugged, picked up his cup of coffee and had a sip. It was the first time he'd really told the truth about it.

"Wow," Ice said. "I'm sorry. Did you ever get tested? Or did she?"

He shook his head. "I didn't. Don't know about her. Maybe she did and didn't tell me. I don't really know. But that was the reason she gave for the breakup."

Just then a phone call came in.

"What's going on?" Levi asked Ice, when her expression changed.

"Remember Di?" Ice asked Levi, while trying to listen to the caller on the other end too.

"Which one? Diamond?"

"No, Dianne from Australia."

"Oh, yeah, sure. What about her?"

"She's in Houston, and she said—wait. Dianne, I'm putting the phone on Speaker."

"Okay," she said, and they heard her taking several deep breaths.

"Are you okay?" Ice asked.

"I'm not sure I am," she said, with a tearful tone. "I was just attacked in my car."

"Uh-oh," Ice said. "Did you call the cops?"

"I would have," she said, "but he, the guy, had a strange message."

"What message?" Levi asked.

"Oh, good. Levi, I'm glad you're there," she said in relief.

"Dianne, are you hurt?"

"No," she said. "Well, yes, but not badly."

"Take it easy," Ice said calmly, her tone measured and comforting. "You're safe now."

"Well, I am now that he's gone," she said, with a hysterical laugh. "Unfortunately he didn't leave fast enough. He cut me."

"How bad?" Levi asked sharply.

"My arm, my shoulder, and a slice across my belly," she said. "None of them look bad. They're just stinging and painful. I'll have to get them checked."

"So tell me again, why call us and not the police?" Levi asked curiously.

"Because the attacker, he had a message for you."

"For me?" Levi asked, standing straight up and walking closer to Ice. "What did he say?"

"He said, it was for—for past sins." Then she started to cry.

"Jesus," he said, staring at Ice. "Did you recognize him, Dianne?"

"Yes," she whispered. "It was Maxwell."

"Maxwell? Maxwell who?"

"Do you remember the guy in Australia, who lost his son on that subway track?"

"That Maxwell?" he said.

"Yes."

"But that makes no sense," he said.

"No," she said. "None of it makes any sense. But it was him. He was right here, attacking me, and something about past sins was your message."

"But we didn't have anything to do with the death of his son."

"No," she said, "but remember? He wanted to come work for you."

"And you really think that's why he's after us?"

She started to cry again.

Noah stared at the three of them in shock. "Hey, Dianne. This is Noah."

"Noah? Do I know you?"

"I work for Levi," he said. "I'm not sure if we've met before or not, but do you want me to come help you?"

There was silence as Levi looked at Noah in surprise.

Noah shrugged. "I don't want to see her alone right now."

"Where are you?" Levi asked Dianne.

"Just give me an address," Noah said to her, "and I'll head your way. What are you doing there anyway?"

"I was at a conference," she said, "and, when I went to the underground parking lot for my rental, that's when he attacked me."

"Sit tight. I'm coming." Noah turned to Ice and said, "Can you get me as much information as you can, then hook me into the conversation while I'm driving there?"

She nodded. "On it," she said. "Dianne, I'll call you right back. Noah is on his way."

"Okay," she said, her voice small, her tone teary. "I just don't know why he used me to get to you."

"Wrong place, wrong time," Levi said.

"I don't think so," she said, her voice getting stronger.

"The way he cut me, it felt like so much more than that."

"Don't worry. We'll get to the bottom of it. Noah is headed your way."

This concludes Book 24 of Heroes for Hire:
Bonaparte's Belle.

Read about Noah's Nemesis: Heroes for Hire, Book 25

Heroes for Hire: Noah's Nemesis (Book #25)

Noah heard the woman's cry for help through Levi's phone, and he was already in the car and moving before anyone could stop him. He hated for any woman to be in distress, and this one sounded devastated. Having helped her once, he was determined to keep her safe, while the team tracked down her attacker.

Dianne was looking forward to her upcoming weekend seminar and even more to the few days with her friend, Ice, at the compound. Dianne wanted to talk over a business idea she was ready to put into place. Being attacked wasn't part of the plan. Neither was Noah. Still she was happy to have him as a babysitter, given the circumstances.

Only someone has a grudge against Levi and sees Dianne as a way to get back at him.

Find Book 25 here!

To find out more visit Dale Mayer's website.

http://smarturl.it/DMSNoah

Other Military Series by Dale Mayer

SEALs of Honor

Heroes for Hire

SEALs of Steel

The K9 Files

The Mavericks

Bullards Battle

Hathaway House

Terkel's Team

Ryland's Reach: Bullard's Battle (Book #1)

Welcome to a new stand-alone but interconnected series from Dale Mayer. This is Bullard's story—and that of his team's. All raw, rough, incredibly capable men who have one goal: to find out who was behind the attack on their leader, before the attacker, or attackers, return to finish the job.

Stay tuned for more nonstop action as the men narrow down their suspects … and find a way to let love back into their own empty lives.

His rescue from the ocean after a horrible plane explosion was his top priority, in any way, shape, or form. A small sailboat and a nurse to do the job was more than Ryland hoped for.

When Tabi somehow drags him and his buddy Garret onboard and surprisingly gets them to a naval ship close by, Ryland figures he'd used up all his luck and his friend's too. Sure enough, those who attacked the plane they were in weren't content to let him slowly die in the ocean. No. Surviving had made him a target all over again.

Tabi isn't expecting her sailing holiday to include the rescue of two badly injured men and then to end with the loss of her beloved sailboat. Her instincts save them, but now she finds it tough to let them go—even as more of Bullard's team members come to them—until it becomes apparent that not only are Bullard and his men still targets ... but she is too.

B ULLARD CHECKED THAT the helicopter was loaded with their bags and that his men were ready to leave.

He walked back one more time, his gaze on Ice. She'd never looked happier, never looked more perfect. His heart ached, but he knew she remained a caring friend and always would be. He opened his arms; she ran into them, and he held her close, whispering, "The offer still stands."

She leaned back and smiled up at him. "Maybe if and when Levi's been gone for a long enough time for me to forget," she said in all seriousness.

"That's not happening. You two, now three, will live long and happy lives together," he said, smiling down at the woman knew to be the most beautiful, inside and out. She would never be his, but he always kept a little corner of his heart open and available, in case she wanted to surprise him and to slide inside.

And then he realized she'd already been a part of his heart all this time. That was a good ten to fifteen years by now. But she kept herself in the friend category, and he understood because she and Levi, partners and now parents, were perfect together.

Bullard reached out and shook Levi's hand. "It was a hell of a blast," he said. "When you guys do a big splash, you really do a *big* splash."

Ice laughed. "A few days at home sounds perfect for me now."

"It looks great," he said, his hands on his hips as he surveyed the people in the massive pool surrounded by the palm trees, all designed and decked out by Ice. Right beside all the war machines that he heartily approved of. He grinned at her. "When are you coming over to visit?" His gaze went to Levi, raising his eyebrows back at her. "You guys should come over for a week or two or three."

"It's not a bad idea," Levi said. "We could use a long holiday, just not yet."

"That sounds familiar." Bullard grinned. "Anyway, I'm off. We'll hit the airport and then pick up the plane and head home." He added, "As always, call if you need me."

Everybody raised a hand as he returned to the helicopter and his buddy who was flying him to the airport. Ice had volunteered to shuttle him there, but he hadn't wanted to take her away from her family or to prolong the goodbye. He hopped inside, waving at everybody as the helicopter lifted. Two of his men, Ryland and Garret, were in the back seats. They always traveled with him.

Bullard would pick up the rest of his men in Australia. He stared down at the compound as he flew overhead. He preferred his compound at home, but damn they'd done a nice job here.

With everybody on the ground screaming goodbye, Bullard sailed over Houston, heading toward the airport. His two men never said a word. They all knew how he felt about Ice. But not one of them would cross that line and say anything. At least not if they expected to still have jobs.

It was one thing to fall in love with another man's woman, but another thing to fall in love with a woman who was so unique, so different, and so absolutely perfect that you knew, just knew, there was no hope of finding anybody else like her. But she and Levi had been together way before Bullard had ever met her, which made it that much more heartbreaking.

Still, he'd turned and looked forward. He had a full roster of jobs himself to focus on when he got home. Part of him was tired of the life; another part of him couldn't wait to head out on the next adventure. He managed to run everything from his command centers in one or two of his locations. He'd spent a lot of time and effort at the second one and kept a full team at both locations, yet preferred to spend most of his time at the old one. It felt more like home to him, and he'd like to be there now, but still had many more days before that could happen.

The helicopter lowered to the tarmac, he stepped out, said his goodbyes and walked across to where his private plane waited. It was one of the things that he loved, being a pilot of both helicopters and airplanes, and owning both birds himself.

That again was another way he and Ice were part of the same team, of the same mind-set. He'd been looking for another woman like Ice for himself, but no such luck. Sure, lots were around for short-term relationships, but most of them couldn't handle his lifestyle or the violence of the world that he lived in. He understood that.

The ones who did had a hard edge to them that he found difficult to live with. Bullard appreciated everybody's being alert and aware, but if there wasn't some softness in the women, they seemed to turn cold all the way through.

As he boarded his small plane, Ryland and Garret following behind, Bullard called out in his loud voice, "Let's go, slow pokes. We've got a long flight ahead of us."

The men grinned, confident Bullard was teasing, as was his usual routine during their off-hours.

"Well, we're ready, not sure about you though ..." Ryland said, smirking.

"We're waiting on you this time," Garret added with a chuckle. "Good thing you're the boss."

Bullard grinned at his two right-hand men. "Isn't that the truth?" He dropped his bags at one of the guys' feet and said, "Stow all this stuff, will you? I want to get our flight path cleared and get the hell out of here."

They'd all enjoyed the break. He tried to get over once a year to visit Ice and Levi and same in reverse. But it was time to get back to business. He started up the engines, got confirmation from the tower. They were heading to Australia for this next job. He really wanted to go straight back to Africa, but it would be a while yet. They'd refuel in Honolulu.

Ryland came in and sat down in the copilot's spot, buckled in, then asked, "You ready?"

Bullard laughed. "When have you ever known me *not* to be ready?" At that, he taxied down the runway. Before long he was up in the air, at cruising level, and heading to Hawaii. "Gotta love these views from up here," Bullard said. "This place is magical."

"It is once you get up above all the smog," he said. "Why Australia again?"

"Remember how we were supposed to check out that newest compound in Australia that I've had my eye on? Besides the alpha team is coming off that ugly job in Sydney. We'll give them a day or two of R&R then head home."

"Right. We could have some equally ugly payback on that job."

Bullard shrugged. "That goes for most of our jobs. It's the life."

"And don't you have enough compounds to look after?"

"Yes I do, but that kid in me still looks to take over the world. Just remember that."

"Better you go home to Africa and look after your first two compounds," Ryland said.

"Maybe," Bullard admitted. "But it seems hard to not continue expanding."

"You need a partner," Ryland said abruptly. "That might ease the savage beast inside. Keep you home more."

"Well, the only one I like," he said, "is married to my best friend."

"I'm sorry about that," Ryland said quietly. "What a shit deal."

"No," Bullard said. "I came on the scene last. They were always meant to be together. Especially now they are a family."

"If you say so," Ryland said.

Bullard nodded. "Damn right, I say so."

And that set the tone for the next many hours. They landed in Hawaii, and while they fueled up everybody got off to stretch their legs by walking around outside a bit as this was a small private airstrip, not exactly full of hangars and tourists. Then they hopped back on board again for takeoff.

"I can fly," Ryland offered as they took off.

"We'll switch in a bit," Bullard said. "Surprisingly, I'm doing okay yet, but I'll let you take her down."

"Yeah, it's still a long flight," Ryland said studying the islands below. It was a stunning view of the area.

"I love the islands here. Sometimes I just wonder about the benefit of, you know, crashing into the sea, coming up on a deserted island, and finding the simple life again," Bullard said with a laugh.

"I hear you," Ryland said. "Every once in a while, I wonder the same."

Several hours later Ryland looked up and said abruptly, "We've made good time considering we've already passed Fiji."

Bullard yawned.

"Let's switch."

Bullard smiled, nodded, and said, "Fine. I'll hand it over to you."

Just then a funny noise came from the engine on the right side.

They looked at each other, and Ryland said, "Uh-oh. That's not good news."

Boom!

And the plane exploded.

Find Bullard's Battle (Book #1) here!

To find out more visit Dale Mayer's website.

smarturl.it/DMSRyland

Damon's Deal: Terkel's Team (Book #1)

Welcome to a brand-new connected series of intrigue, betrayal, and ... murder, from the *USA Today* best-selling author Dale Mayer. A series with all the elements you've come to love, plus so much more... including psychics!

A betrayal from within has Terkel frantic to protect those he can, as his team falls one by one, from a murderous killer he helped create.

ICE POURED HERSELF a coffee and sat down at the compound's massive dining room table with the others. When her phone rang, she smiled at the number displayed. "Hey, Terk. How're you doing?" She put the call on Speakerphone.

"I'm okay," Terkel said, his voice distracted and tight.

"Terk?" Merk called from across the table. He got up and walked closer and sat across from Levi. "You don't sound too good, brother. What's up?"

"I'm fine," Terk said. "Or I will be. Right now, things are blown to shit."

"As in literally?" Merk asked.

"The entire group," Terk said, "they're all gone. I had a solid team of eight, and they're all gone."

"Dead?"

Several others stood to join them, gathered around Ice's phone. Levi stepped forward, his hand on Ice's shoulder. "Terk? Are they all dead?"

"No." Terk took a deep breath. "I'm not making sense. I'm sorry."

"Take it easy," Ice said, her voice calm and reassuring. "What do you mean, *they're all gone?*"

"All their abilities are gone," he said. "Something's happened to them. Somebody has deliberately removed whatever super senses they could utilize—or what we have been utilizing for the last ten years for the government." His tone was bitter. "When the US gov recently closed us down, they promised that our black ops department would never rise again, but I didn't expect them to attack us personally."

"What are you talking about?" Merk said in alarm, standing up now to stare at Ice's phone. "Are you in danger?"

"Maybe? I don't know," Terk said. "I need to find out exactly what the hell's going on."

"What can we do to help?" Ice asked.

Terk gave a broken laugh. "That's not why I'm calling. Well, it is, but it isn't."

Ice looked at Merk, who frowned, as he shook his head. Ice knew he and the others had heard Terk's stressed out tone and the completely confusing bits and pieces coming from his mouth. Ice said, "Terk, you're not making sense again. Take a breath and explain. Please. You're scaring me."

Terk took a long slow deep breath. "Tell Stone to open the gate," he said. "She's out there."

"Who's out there?" Levi asked, hopped up, looked outside, and shrugged.

"She's coming up the road now. You have to let her in."

"Who? Why?"

"*Because*," he said, "she's also harnessed with C-4."

"Jesus," Levi said, bolting to display the camera feeds to the big screen in the room. "Is it live?"

"It is, and she's been sent to you."

"Well, that's an interesting move," Ice said, her voice sharp, activating her comm to connect to Stone in the control room. "Who's after us?"

"I think it's rebels within the Iranian government. But it could be our own government. I don't know anymore," Terk snapped. "I also don't know how they got her so close to you. Or how they pinned your connection to me," he said. "I've been very careful."

"We can look after ourselves," Ice said immediately. "But who is this woman to you?"

"She's pregnant," he said, "so that adds to the intensity here."

"Understood. So who is the father? Is he connected somehow?"

There was silence on the other end.

Merk said, "Terk, talk to us."

"She's carrying my baby," Terk replied, his voice heavy.

Merk, his expression grim, looked at Ice, her face mirroring his shock. He asked, "How do you know her, Terk?"

"Brother, you don't understand," Terk said. "I've never met this woman before in my life." And, with that, the phone went dead.

Find Terkel's Team (Book #1) here!

To find out more visit Dale Mayer's website.

smarturl.it/DMSTTDamon

Author's Note

Thank you for reading Bonaparte's Belle: Heroes for Hire, Book 24! If you enjoyed the book, please take a moment and leave a short review.

Dear reader,

I love to hear from readers, and you can contact me at my website: www.dalemayer.com or at my Facebook author page. To be informed of new releases and special offers, sign up for my newsletter or follow me on BookBub. And if you are interested in joining Dale Mayer's Reader Group, here is the Facebook sign up page. https://smarturl.it/DaleMayerFBGroup

Cheers,
Dale Mayer

Your THREE Free Books Are Waiting!

Grab your copy of SEALs of Honor Books 1 – 3 for free!

Meet Mason, Hawk and Dane. *Brave, badass warriors who serve their country with honor and love their women to the limits of life and death.*

DOWNLOAD your copy right now! Just tell me where to send it.

www.smarturl.it/DaleHonorFreeBundle

About the Author

Dale Mayer is a *USA Today* best-selling author, best known for her SEALs military romances, her Psychic Visions series, and her Lovely Lethal Garden cozy series. Her contemporary romances are raw and full of passion and emotion (Broken But ... Mending series). Her thrillers will keep you guessing (By Death series), and her romantic comedies will keep you giggling (*It's a Dog's Life*, a stand-alone novella; and the Broken Protocols series, starring Charming Marvin, the cat).

Dale honors the stories that come to her—and some of them are crazy and break all the rules and cross multiple genres!

To go with her fiction, she also writes nonfiction in many different fields, with books available on résumé writing, companion gardening, and the US mortgage system. She has recently published her Career Essentials series. All her books are available in print and ebook format.

Connect with Dale Mayer Online

Dale's Website – www.dalemayer.com

Twitter – @DaleMayer

Facebook – facebook.com/DaleMayer.author

BookBub – bookbub.com/authors/dale-mayer

Also by Dale Mayer

Published Adult Books:

Bullard's Battle

Ryland's Reach, Book 1

Cain's Cross, Book 2

Eton's Escape, Book 3

Garret's Gambit, Book 4

Kano's Keep, Book 5

Fallon's Flaw, Book 6

Quinn's Quest, Book 7

Bullard's Beauty, Book 8

Bullard's Best, Book 9

Terkel's Team

Damon's Deal, Book 1

Kate Morgan

Simon Says… Hide, Book 1

Hathaway House

Aaron, Book 1

Brock, Book 2

Cole, Book 3

Denton, Book 4

Psychic Vision Series

Tuesday's Child

Hide 'n Go Seek

Maddy's Floor

Garden of Sorrow

Knock Knock...

Rare Find

Eyes to the Soul

Now You See Her

Shattered

Into the Abyss

Seeds of Malice

Eye of the Falcon

Itsy-Bitsy Spider

Unmasked

Deep Beneath

From the Ashes

Stroke of Death

Ice Maiden

Snap, Crackle...

Psychic Visions Books 1–3

Psychic Visions Books 4–6

Psychic Visions Books 7–9

By Death Series

Touched by Death

Haunted by Death

Chilled by Death

By Death Books 1–3

Broken Protocols – Romantic Comedy Series

Cat's Meow

Cat's Pajamas

Cat's Cradle

Cat's Claus

Broken Protocols 1-4

Broken and... Mending

Skin

Scars

Scales (of Justice)

Broken but... Mending 1-3

Glory

Genesis

Tori

Celeste

Glory Trilogy

Biker Blues

Morgan: Biker Blues, Volume 1

Cash: Biker Blues, Volume 2

SEALs of Honor

Mason: SEALs of Honor, Book 1

Hawk: SEALs of Honor, Book 2

Dane: SEALs of Honor, Book 3

Swede: SEALs of Honor, Book 4

Shadow: SEALs of Honor, Book 5

Cooper: SEALs of Honor, Book 6

Heroes for Hire

Heroes for Hire, Books 10–12

Heroes for Hire, Books 13–15

SEALs of Steel

Badger: SEALs of Steel, Book 1

Erick: SEALs of Steel, Book 2

Cade: SEALs of Steel, Book 3

Talon: SEALs of Steel, Book 4

Laszlo: SEALs of Steel, Book 5

Geir: SEALs of Steel, Book 6

Jager: SEALs of Steel, Book 7

The Final Reveal: SEALs of Steel, Book 8

SEALs of Steel, Books 1–4

SEALs of Steel, Books 5–8

SEALs of Steel, Books 1–8

The Mavericks

Kerrick, Book 1

Griffin, Book 2

Jax, Book 3

Beau, Book 4

Asher, Book 5

Ryker, Book 6

Miles, Book 7

Nico, Book 8

Keane, Book 9

Lennox, Book 10

Gavin, Book 11

Shane, Book 12

Diesel, Book 13

Jerricho, Book 14

The Mavericks, Books 1–2

The Mavericks, Books 3–4

The Mavericks, Books 5–6

The Mavericks, Books 7–8

The Mavericks, Books 9–10

The Mavericks, Books 11–12

Collections

Dare to Be You...

Dare to Love...

Dare to be Strong...

RomanceX3

Standalone Novellas

It's a Dog's Life

Riana's Revenge

Second Chances

Published Young Adult Books:

Family Blood Ties Series

Vampire in Denial

Vampire in Distress

Vampire in Design

Vampire in Deceit

Vampire in Defiance

Vampire in Conflict

Vampire in Chaos

Vampire in Crisis

Vampire in Control

Vampire in Charge

Family Blood Ties Set 1–3

Family Blood Ties Set 1–5

Family Blood Ties Set 4–6

Family Blood Ties Set 7–9

Sian's Solution, A Family Blood Ties Series Prequel
Novelette

Design series

Dangerous Designs

Deadly Designs

Darkest Designs

Design Series Trilogy

Standalone

In Cassie's Corner

Gem Stone (a Gemma Stone Mystery)

Time Thieves

Published Non-Fiction Books:

Career Essentials

Career Essentials: The Résumé

Career Essentials: The Cover Letter

Career Essentials: The Interview

Career Essentials: 3 in 1

Made in the USA
Middletown, DE
05 August 2021